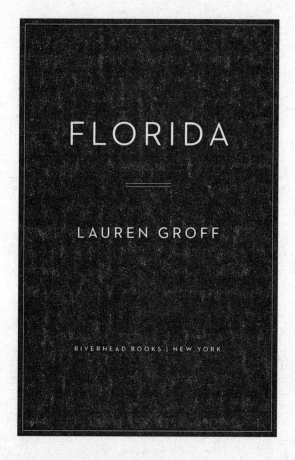

FLORIDA

LAUREN GROFF

RIVERHEAD BOOKS | NEW YORK

RIVERHEAD BOOKS
An imprint of Penguin Random House LLC
penguinrandomhouse.com

Thank you to the editors of the journals where these stories were first published:
The New Yorker for "Ghosts and Empties," "Dogs Go Wolf," "The Midnight Zone,"
"Flower Hunters," and "Above and Below"; *Five Points* for "At the Round Earth's Imagined
Corners"; *Subtropics* for "Eyewall"; *American Short Fiction* for "For the God of Love, for the
Love of God"; *Tin House* for "Salvador"; *Esquire* for "Snake Stories"; and *Granta* for an
abridged version of "Yport." Thank you to the editors of the anthologies *Best American
Short Stories* (2014, 2016, and 2017), *100 Years of the Best American Short Stories*, and
The PEN/O. Henry Prize Stories (2012).

Library of Congress Cataloging-in-Publication Data

Names: Groff, Lauren, author.
Title: Florida / Lauren Groff.
Description: New York : Riverhead Books, 2018.
Identifiers: LCCN 2017042916 | ISBN 9781594634512 (hardcover) |
ISBN 9780698405141 (ebook)
Classification: LCC PS3607.R6344 A6 2018 | DDC 813/.6—dc23
LC record available at https://lccn.loc.gov/2017042916
p.   cm.

First Riverhead hardcover edition: June 2018
First Riverhead trade paperback edition: May 2019
Riverhead trade paperback ISBN: 9781594634529

Printed in the United States of America
1   3   5   7   9   10   8   6   4   2

Book design by Gretchen Achilles

For Heath

and get lost in a swamp. Groff's depictions aren't always pretty, but they'll keep you turning the pages—and not just for the breeze."

—People

"[A] transcendent writer . . . [Florida] isn't a short-story collection so much as an ecosystem."

—The Atlantic

"[Groff] stakes her claim to being Florida's unofficial poet laureate, as Joan Didion was for California."

—The Washington Post

"Superlative collection—seriously, there's not a dud in the bunch. . . . Groff is an extra terrific writer, as ever. . . . Having followed an astonishing, astonishingly accessible novel with such an outstanding, accessible collection, Groff is surely poised to topple the tiny monkeys in charge of deciding that the perceived realm of the feminine isn't sufficiently deep."

—The Boston Globe

"Taken together, the stories have the feel of autobiography, although, as in a Salvador Dalí painting, their emotional disclosures are encrypted in phantasmagoria. . . . The sentences indigenous to Florida are gorgeously weird and limber."

—The New Yorker

"Brooding, inventive and often moving short stories . . . In Groff's trademark zigzagging storytelling style, revelations ricochet between pages—and sometimes even within single sentences. . . . Groff, through her own acrobatic style, attests to the benefits of a firm grounding in grammar and vocabulary. Lots of things go south fast in the stories collected in Florida—like marriages, careers and the weather—but throughout, Groff's gifts as a writer just keep soaring higher and higher."

—Fresh Air (NPR)

"Groff's desire seems to be to show—in a frequently funny, sometimes painful and always deeply sensitive way—that women and children are often stronger than we tend to think, and that the Earth is more fragile than we usually allow ourselves to understand."

—San Francisco Chronicle

"Easily the year's best story collection . . . These indelibly vivid tales read like inoculations against cynicism."

—Vogue

"[Groff's stories] take on an inexplicably cohesive form with a sad-, beautiful- and naked-ness that reverberates in the mind long after the book is shut."   —*The Atlanta Journal-Constitution*

"Groff's language is, as always, gorgeous and precise. Her ability to map the inner contours of characters who seem to exist entirely in extremis—and, almost entirely, within a fragile shell of feigned competence and normalcy—is remarkable. Her Florida is a frightening place that bends (solely through the eyes and experiences of her characters) into a discomfortingly modern Southern Gothic tradition. Her stories—all of them—are haunted."   —*Books* (NPR)

"Slime mold, a father killed by snake venom, a mother haunted by a deadly panther, and half-feral little girls abandoned on an island—these bizarre happenings could be set only in the Sunshine State, and be written only by Groff, the Gabriel García Márquez of Gainesville. Reading as required as insect repellent in a swamp."
                —*O, the Oprah Magazine*

"Groff is still on-brand. Her writing about relationships rarely sticks within the narrow, Updike-ian confines of domestic dysfunction, though. Even in short stories, she prefers broader canvases, and much of *Florida* is filled with hurricanes and other violent storms that run parallel to the personal crises she describes. . . . Straightforward but moody and metaphorical—magical realism without the sparkle and sense of wonder."   —*Los Angeles Times*

"The landscapes in [*Florida*] are silty, rich, sun-bleached, cold as stone. They are strong characters of their own that will not be ignored."   —*Electric Literature*

"Impossible to put down."   —*Vox*

"Groff's mythic almost gothic stories about Florida and domesticity and entrapment took me right back to the Brontë sisters. . . . Masterfully made."   —*Literary Hub*

"You're helpless to the power—the sheer virtuosity—of Groff's evocative prose."   —*Entertainment Weekly*

CONTENTS

GHOSTS AND EMPTIES

I have somehow become a woman who yells, and because I do not want to be a woman who yells, whose little children walk around with frozen, watchful faces, I have taken to lacing on my running shoes after dinner and going out into the twilit streets for a walk, leaving the undressing and sluicing and reading and singing and tucking in of the boys to my husband, a man who does not yell.

The neighborhood goes dark as I walk, and a second neighborhood unrolls atop the daytime one. We have few streetlights, and those I pass under make my shadow frolic; it lags behind me, gallops to my feet, gambols on ahead. The only other illumination is from the windows in the houses I pass and the moon that orders me to look up, look up! Feral cats dart underfoot, bird-of-paradise flowers poke out of the shadows, smells are exhaled into the air: oak dust, slime mold, camphor.

Northern Florida is cold in January and I walk fast for warmth but also because, though the neighborhood is antique—huge Victorian houses radiating outward into 1920s bungalows, then mid-century modern ranches at the edges—it's imperfectly safe. There was a rape a month ago, a jogger in her fifties pulled into the azaleas; and, a week ago, a pack of loose pit bulls ran down a mother with a baby in her stroller and mauled both, though not to death. It's not the dogs' fault, it's the owners' fault! dog lovers shouted on the neighborhood email list, but those dogs were sociopaths. When the suburbs were built, in the seventies, the historic houses in the center of town were abandoned to graduate students who heated beans over Bunsen burners on the heart-pine floors and sliced apartments out of ballrooms. When neglect and humidity caused the houses to rot and droop and develop rusty scales, there was a second abandonment, to poor people, squatters. We moved here ten years ago because our house was cheap and had virgin-lumber bones, and because I decided that if I had to live in the South, with its boiled peanuts and its Spanish moss dangling like armpit hair, at least I wouldn't barricade myself with my whiteness in a gated community. Isn't it . . . dicey? people our parents' age would say, grimacing, when we told them where we lived, and it took all my willpower not to say, Do you mean black, or just poor? Because it was both.

White middle-classness has since infected the neighborhood, though, and now everything is frenzied with renovation. In the past few years, the black people have mostly withdrawn. The homeless stayed for a while, because our neighborhood abuts Bo Diddley Plaza, where, until recently, churches handed out food and God, and where Occupy rolled in like a tide and claimed the right to sleep there, then grew tired of being dirty and rolled out, leaving behind a human flotsam of the homeless in sleeping bags. During our first months in the house, we hosted a homeless couple we only ever saw slinking off in the dawn: at dusk, they would silently lift off the latticework to the crawl space under our house and then sleep there, their roof our bedroom floor, and when we got up in the middle of the night, we tried to walk softly because it felt rude to step inches above the face of a dreaming person.

On my nighttime walks, the neighbors' lives reveal themselves, the lit windows domestic aquariums. At times, I'm the silent witness to fights that look like slow-dancing without music. It is astonishing how people live, the messes they sustain, the delicious whiffs of cooking that carry to the street, the holiday decorations that slowly seep into daily decor. All January, I watched a Christmas bouquet of roses on one mantel diminish until the flowers were a blighted shrivel and the water green scum, a huge Santa on a stick still beaming merrily out of the ruins. Window after window nears, freezes with its blue fog of television light or its couple hunched over a supper of pizza, holds as I pass, then slides into the forgotten. I think of the

3

way water gathers as it slips down an icicle's length, pauses to build its glossy drop, becomes too fat to hang on, plummets down.

There is one mostly windowless place in the neighborhood that I love nevertheless, because it houses nuns. There used to be six nuns there, but attrition happened, as it does with very old ladies, and now there are only three kindly sisters squeaking around that immense space in their sensible shoes. A realtor friend told us that when it was built in the 1950s, a bomb shelter was lowered into the porous limestone of the backyard, and during sleepless nights, when my body is in bed but my brain is still out walking in the dark, I like to imagine the nuns in full regalia in their shelter, singing hymns and spinning on a stationary bike to keep the lightbulb sputtering on, while, aboveground, all has been blasted black, and rusted hinges rasp the wind.

Because the nights are so cold, I share the streets with few people. There's a young couple who jog at a pace slightly slower than my fast walk. I follow them, listening to their patter of wedding plans and fights with friends. Once I forgot myself and laughed at something they said and their faces owled, unnerved, back at me, then they trotted faster and took the first turn they found and I let them disappear into the black.

There's an elegant, tall woman who walks a Great

Dane the color of dryer lint; I am afraid that the woman is unwell because she walks rigidly, her face pulsing as if intermittently electrified by pain. I sometimes imagine how, should I barrel around a corner to find her slumped on the ground, I would drape her over her dog, smack his withers, and watch as he, with his great dignity, carried her home.

There is a boy of fifteen or so, tremendously fat, whose shirt is always off and who is always on the treadmill on his glassed-in porch. No matter how many times I find myself striding past his window, there he is, his footsteps pounding so hard I can hear them from two blocks away. Because all the lights are on inside the house, to him there is nothing beyond the black in the window, and I wonder if he watches his reflection the way I watch him, if he sees how with each step his stomach ripples as if it were a pond into which someone had tossed a fist-sized stone.

There's the shy muttering homeless lady, a collector of cans, who hoists her clanging bags on the back of her bicycle and uses the old concrete blocks in front of the grander houses to mount her ride; the waft of her makes me think of the wealthy southern dames in dark silk who once used those blocks to climb into their carriages, emitting a similarly intimate feminine stink. Hygiene may have changed with time, but human bodies have not.

There's the man who hisses nasties as he stands under the light outside a bodega with bars over its windows. I put on my don't-fuck-with-me face, and he has yet to do more than hiss, but there is a part of me that is more than ready, that wants to use what's building up.

Sometimes I think I see the stealthy couple who lived under our house, the particular angle of his solicitousness, his hand on her back, but when I come closer it is only a papaya tree bent over a rain barrel or two boys smoking in the bushes, turning wary as I pass.

And then there's the therapist who every night sits at his desk in the study of his Victorian, which looks like a rotting galleon. One of his patients caught the therapist in bed with the patient's own wife; the patient kept a loaded shotgun in his car. The wife died in coitus and the therapist survived with a bullet still in his hip, which makes him lurch when he gets up to pour himself more Scotch. There are rumors that he visits the cuckolded murderer in prison every week, though whether his motive is kindness or crowing remains shadowy, but it's not as if motives could ever be pure. My husband and I had just moved in when the murder occurred; we were scraping rotting paint off the oak moldings in our dining room when the gunshots splattered the air, but of course we believed they were fireworks lit by the kids who lived a few houses down.

As I walk, I see strangers but also people I know. I look up in the beginning of February to see a close friend in a pink leotard in her window, stretching, but then, with a zip of understanding, I realize that she isn't stretching, she is drying her legs, and the leotard is, in fact, her body, pinked from the hot shower. Even though I visited her in the hospital when both of her boys were born, held the newborns in my arms when they still smelled of her, saw the raw cesarean split, it isn't until I watch her drying herself that I understand that she is a sexual being, and then the next time we speak I can't help blushing and enduring images of her in extreme sexual positions. Mostly, however, I see the mothers I know in glimpses, bent like shepherdess crooks, scanning the floor for tiny Legos or half-chewed grapes or the people they once were, slumped in the corners.

It's too much, it's too much, I shout at my husband some nights when I come home, and he looks at me, afraid, this giant gentle man, and sits up in bed over his computer and says, softly, I don't think you've walked it off yet, sweets, you may want to take one more loop. I go out again, furious, because the streets become more dangerous this late at night, and how dare he suggest risk like this to me, when I have proved myself vulnerable; but then again, perhaps my warm house has become more dangerous as well. During the day, while my sons are in school, I can't stop reading about the disaster of the world, the glaciers dying like living creatures, the great Pacific trash gyre, the hundreds of unrecorded deaths of species, millennia snuffed out as if they were not precious. I read and savagely mourn, as if reading could somehow sate this hunger for grief, instead of what it does, which is fuel it.

have mostly stopped caring where I walk, but I try to be at the Duck Pond every night when the Christmas lights, forgotten for weeks now, click off and the pond erupts, the frogs launching into their syncopated song. Our pair of black swans would shout at the frogs with their brass voices as if to shut them up, but, outnumbered, the birds would soon give up and climb the island in the center of the pond and twine their necks together to sleep. The swans had four cygnets last spring, sweet cheeping puffs that were the delight of my little boys, who tossed dog food at them every day, until one morning, while the swans were distracted by our food, one cygnet gave a choked peep, bobbed, then went down; it came up again but across the pond, in the paws of an otter that ate it in small bites, floating serenely on its back. The otter got one more cygnet before the wildlife service arrived to scoop up the remaining two, but it was later reported in the neighborhood newsletter that the tiny swan hearts had given out in fear. The parent swans floated for months, inconsolable. Perhaps this is a projection: as they are both black swans and parents, they are already pre-feathered in mourning.

On Valentine's Day, I see red and white lights flashing from afar at the nunnery and walk faster in the hope that the nuns are having a love party, a disco rager, but instead I see an ambulance drive away, and the next day my fears are confirmed; the nuns have been further diminished, to two. Withholding erotic pleasure for the glory of God seems an anachronism in our hedonistic age, and, with their frailty and the hugeness of the house they rattle around in, it has been decided that the remaining nuns must decamp. I come to watch them the night they leave, expecting a moving truck, but there are only a few leather suitcases and a box or two in the back of the nuns' station wagon. Their wrinkled faces droop with relief as they drive off.

The cold lingers on into March. It has been a hard winter for everyone, though not as terrible as in the North, and I think of my friends and family up there with their dirty walls of snow and try to remember that the camellias and peach trees and dogwoods and oranges are all abloom here, even in the dark. I smell the jasmine potent in my hair the next morning, the way I used to smell cigarette smoke and sweat after going to a nightclub, back when I was young and could do such unthinkable things. There is a vernacular style of architecture called Cracker, which is not meant to cause offense, all porches and high ceilings; and by the middle of March, one of the oldest Cracker houses in north central Florida is being renovated. The façade is preserved, but the rest is gutted. Night by night, I see what remains of the house as daily it is stripped away, until one night the house has entirely vanished: that morning it collapsed on a worker, who survived, like Buster Keaton, by standing in the window as the structure fell. I study the hole where a humble and unremarked history stood for so long, a house that watched the town press up, then grow around it, and I think of the construction worker who walked out of the collapse unhurt, what he was imagining. I think I know. One night just before Christmas I came home late after a walk and my husband was in the bathroom and I flipped open his computer and saw what I saw there, a conversation not meant for me, a snip of flesh that was not his, and without letting him know I was in the house, I about-faced and went out again and walked until it was too cold to walk, until just before dawn, when the dew could easily have been ice.

Now, while I stand before the collapsed house, the woman with the Great Dane slides by through the dark, and I notice how aggressively pale she has become, so skinny her cheeks must touch inside her mouth, her wig askew to show a rind of scalp above the bangs. If she, in turn, notices the particular dark spike of my unrest, she says only a soft good night and her dog looks at me with a kind of human compassion, and together they move off, stately and gentle, into the black.

Most changes are not so swift as the fallen house, and I notice how much weight the boy in his glassed-in sunporch has lost only when I realize from the sound of his footsteps that he's no longer walking on his treadmill but running, and I look at him closely for the first time in a long time, my dear flabby friend whom I took for granted, and see a transformation so astonishing it's as if a maiden had turned into a birch tree or a stream. During these few months, this overweight child has become a slender man with pectoral rosebuds on his chest, sweating, smiling at himself in the glass, and I yelp aloud because of the swiftness of youth, these gorgeous changes that insist that not everything is decaying faster than we can love it.

I walk on, and as the boy's trotting noises fade I hear a disquieting constant sound that I can't place. It is a sticky night: I shed my jacket last week, and it is only gradually that I understand that the noise is coming from the first air conditioner turned on for the year. Soon they'll all be on, crouched like trolls under the windows, their collective tuneless hum drowning out the night birds and frogs, and time will leap forward and the night will grow more and more reluctant to descend and, in the cool linger of twilight, people longing for real air after the sickly fake cold all day will come out and I will no longer have my dangerous dark streets to myself. There's a pleasant smell like campfires in the air, and I think that the old turpentine-pine forests that ring the city must be on fire, which happens once a year or so, and I wonder about all those poor birds seared out of their sleep and into the disorienting darkness. I discover the next morning that it was worse, a controlled burn over the acres where dozens of the homeless had been living in a tent city, and I walk down to look, but it's all great oaks, lonely and blackened from the waist down in a plain of steaming charcoal. When I return and see the six-foot fences around Bo Diddley Plaza that had gone up that same night for construction, or so the signs say, it is clear that it is part of a larger plan, balletically executed. I stand squinting in the daylight wanting to yell, looking to find a displaced person. Please, I think, please let my couple come by, let me see their faces at last, let me take their arms. I want to make them sandwiches and give them blankets and tell them that it's okay, that they can live under my house. Later, I'm glad I never found them, when I remember that it is not a kind thing to tell human beings that they can live under your house.

The week of heat proves temporary, a false start to the season. The weather again turns so clammy and cold that nobody else comes out, and I shiver as I walk, until I escape my chill by going into the drugstore for Epsom salts to soak my walking away. It is shocking to enter the dazzling color, the ferocious heat after the chilly gray scale; to travel hundreds of miles over the cracked sidewalks and sparse palmettos and black path-crossing cats I dart away from, into this abundance with its aisles of gaudy trash and useless wrapping and plastic pull tabs that will one day end up in the throat of the earth's last sea turtle. I find myself limping, and the limp morphs into a kind of pained bopping because the music dredges up elementary school, when my parents were, astonishingly, younger than I am now, and that one long summer they listened on repeat to Paul Simon singing over springy African drums about a trip with a son, the human trampoline, the window in the heart. It is both too much and too little, and I leave without the salts because I am not ready for such easy absolution as this. I can't.

And so I walk and I walk, and at some point, near the wildly singing frogs, I look up, and out of the darkness, a stun: the new possessor of the old nunnery has installed uplighting, not on the aesthetic blank of the cube but, rather, on the ardent live oak in front of it, so old and so broad it spreads out over a half acre. I've always known the tree was there, and my children have often swung on its low branches and from the bark plucked out ferns and epiphytes with which to adorn my head. But the tree has never before announced itself fully as the colossus it is, with its branches that are so heavy they grow toward the ground then touch and grow upward again; and thus, elbowing itself up, it brings to mind a woman at the kitchen table, knuckling her chin and dreaming. I stand shocked by its beauty, and as I look, I imagine the swans on their island seeing the bright spark in the night and feeling their swan hearts moved. I heard that they have started building a nest again, though how they can bear it after all they've lost I do not know.

I hope they understand, my sons, both now and in the future just materializing in the dark, that all these hours their mother has been walking so swiftly away from them I have not been gone, that my spirit, hours ago, slipped back into the house and crept into the room where their early-rising father had already fallen asleep, usually before eight p.m., and that I touched this gentle man whom I love so desperately and somehow fear so much, touched him on the pulse in his temple and felt his dreams, which are too distant for the likes of me; and I climbed the creaking old stairs and at the top split in two, and heading into the boys' separate rooms, I slid through the crack under the doors and curled myself on the pillows to breathe into me the breath that my children breathed out. Every pause between the end of one breath and the beginning of the next is long; then again, nothing is not always in transition. Soon, tomorrow, the boys will be men, then the men will leave the house, and my husband and I will look at each other crouching under the weight of all that we wouldn't or couldn't yell, as well as all those hours outside walking together, my body, my shadow, and the moon. It is terribly true, even if the truth does not comfort, that if you look at the moon for long enough night after night, as I have, you will see that the old cartoons are correct, that the moon is, in fact, laughing. But it is not laughing at us, we lonely humans, who are far too small and our lives far too fleeting for it to give us any notice at all.

AT THE ROUND EARTH'S
IMAGINED CORNERS

J ude was born in a Cracker-style house at the edge of a swamp that boiled with unnamed species of reptiles. Few people lived in the center of Florida then. Air-conditioning was for the rich, and the rest compensated with high ceilings, sleeping porches, attic fans. Jude's father was a herpetologist at the university, and if snakes hadn't slipped their way into their hot house, his father would have filled it with them anyway. Coils of rattlers sat in formaldehyde on the windowsills. Writhing knots of reptiles lived in the coops out back, where his mother had once tried to raise chickens. At an early age, Jude learned to keep a calm heart when touching fanged things. He was barely walking when his mother came into the kitchen to find a coral snake chasing its red and yellow tail around his wrist. His father was watching from across the room, laughing. His mother was a Yankee, a

Presbyterian. She was always weary; she battled the house's mold and humidity and devilish reek of snakes without help. His father wouldn't allow a black person through his doors, and they didn't have the money to hire a white woman. Jude's mother was afraid of scaly creatures, and sang hymns in the attempt to keep them out. When she was pregnant with Jude's sister, she came into the bathroom to take a cool bath one August night and, without her glasses, missed the three-foot albino alligator her husband had stored in the bathtub. The next morning, she was gone. She returned a week later. And after Jude's sister was born dead, a perfect petal of a baby, his mother never stopped singing under her breath.

Noise of the war grew louder. At last, it became impossible to ignore. Jude was two. His mother pressed his father's new khaki suit and then Jude's father's absence filled the house with a kind of cool breeze. He was flying cargo planes in France. Jude thought of scaly creatures flapping great wings midair, his father angrily riding.

While Jude napped the first day they were alone in the house, his mother tossed all of the jars of dead snakes into the swamp and neatly beheaded the living ones with a hoe. She bobbed her hair with gardening shears. Within a week, she had moved them ninety miles to the beach. When she thought he was asleep on the first night in the new house, she went down to the water's edge in the moonlight and screwed her feet into the sand. It seemed that the glossed edge of the ocean was chewing her up to her knees. Jude held his breath, anguished. One big wave rolled past her shoulders, and when it receded, she was whole again.

This was a new world, full of dolphins that slid up the coastline in shining arcs. Jude loved the wedges of pelicans ghosting overhead, the mad dig after periwinkles that disappeared deeper into the wet sand. He kept count in his head when they hunted for them, and when they came home, he told his mother that they had dug up four hundred and sixty-one. She looked at him unblinking behind her glasses and counted the creatures aloud. When she finished, she washed her hands for a long time at the sink.

You like numbers, she said at last, turning around.

Yes, he said. And she smiled, and a kind of gentle shine came from her that startled him. He felt it seep into him, settle in his bones. She kissed him on the crown and put him to bed, and when he woke in the middle of the night to find her next to him, he tucked his hand under her chin, where it stayed until morning.

He began to sense that the world worked in ways beyond him, that he was only grasping at threads of a greater fabric. Jude's mother started a bookstore. Because women couldn't buy land in Florida for themselves, his uncle, a roly-poly little man who looked nothing like Jude's father, bought the store with her money and signed the place over to her. His mother began wearing suits that showed her décolletage and taking her glasses off before boarding the streetcars, so that the eyes she turned to the public were soft. Instead of singing Jude to sleep as she had in the snake house, she read to him. She read Shakespeare, Neruda, Rilke, and he fell asleep with their cadences and the sea's slow rhythm entwined in his head.

Jude loved the bookstore; it was a bright place that smelled of new paper. Lonely war brides came with their prams and left with an armful of Modern Library classics, sailors on leave wandered in only to exit, charmed, with sacks of books pressed to their chests. After-hours, his mother would turn off the lights and open the back door to the black folks who waited patiently there, the dignified man in his watch cap who loved Galsworthy, the fat woman who worked as a maid and read a novel every day. Your father would squeal. Well, foo on him, his mother said to Jude, looking so fierce she erased the last traces in his mind of the tremulous woman she'd been.

One morning just before dawn, he was alone on the beach when he saw a vast metallic breaching a hundred yards offshore. The submarine looked at him with its single periscope eye and slipped silently under again.

Jude told nobody. He kept this dangerous knowledge inside him, where it tightened and squeezed, but where it couldn't menace the greater world.

Jude's mother brought in a black woman named Sandy to help her with housework and to watch Jude while she was at the store. Sandy and his mother became friends, and some nights he would awaken to laughter from the veranda and come out to find his mother and Sandy in the night breeze off the ocean. They drank sloe gin fizzes and ate lemon cake, which Sandy was careful to keep on hand even though by then sugar was getting scarce. They let him have a slice, and he'd fall asleep on Sandy's broad lap, sweetness souring on his tongue, and in his ears the exhalation of the ocean, the sound of women's voices.

At six, he discovered multiplication all by himself, crouched over an anthill in the hot sun. If twelve ants left the anthill per minute, he thought, that meant seven hundred twenty departures per hour, an immensity of leaving, of return. He ran into the bookstore, wordless with happiness. When he buried his head in his mother's lap, the women chatting with her at the counter mistook his sobbing for something sad.

I'm sure the boy misses his father, one lady said, intending to be kind.

No, his mother said. She alone understood his bursting heart and scratched his scalp gently. But something shifted in Jude; and he thought with wonder of his father, of whom his mother had spoken so rarely in all these years that the man himself had faded. Jude could barely recall the rasp of scale on scale and the darkness of the Cracker house in the swamp, curtains closed to keep out the hot, stinking sun.

But it was as if the well-meaning lady had summoned him, and Jude's father came home. He sat, immense and rough-cheeked, in the middle of the sunroom. Jude's mother sat nervously opposite him on the divan, angling her knees away from his. The boy played quietly with his wooden train on the floor. Sandy came in with fresh cookies, and when she went back into the kitchen, his father said something so softly Jude couldn't catch it. His mother stared at his father for a long time, then got up and went to the kitchen, and the screen door slapped, and the boy never saw Sandy again.

While his mother was gone, Jude's father said, We're going home.

Jude couldn't look at his father. The space in the air where he existed was too heavy and dark. He pushed his train around the ankle of a chair. Come here, his father said, and slowly, the boy stood and went to his father's knee.

A big hand flicked out, and Jude's face burned from

ear to mouth. He fell down but didn't cry out. He sucked in blood from his nose and felt it pool behind his throat.

His mother ran in and picked him up. What happened? she shouted, and his father said in his cold voice, Boy's timid. Something's wrong with him.

He keeps things in. He's shy, said his mother, and carried Jude away. He could feel her trembling as she washed the blood from his face. His father came into the bathroom and she said through her teeth, Don't you ever touch him again.

He said, I won't have to.

His mother lay beside Jude until he fell asleep, but he woke to the moon through the automobile's windshield and his parents' jagged profiles staring ahead into the tunnel of the dark road.

The house by the swamp filled with snakes again. The uncle who had helped his mother with the bookstore was no longer welcome, although he was the only family his father had. Jude's mother cooked a steak and potatoes every night but wouldn't eat. She became a bone, a blade. She sat in her housedress on the porch rocker, her hair slick with sweat. Jude stood near her and spoke the old sonnets into her ear. She pulled him to her side and put her face between his shoulder and neck, and when she blinked, her wet eyelashes tickled him, and he knew not to move away.

His father had begun, on the side, selling snakes to zoos and universities. He vanished for two, three nights in a row, and returned with clothes full of smoke and sacks of rattlers and blacksnakes. He'd been gone for two nights when his mother packed her blue cardboard suitcase with Jude's things on one side and hers on the other. She said nothing, but gave herself away with humming. They walked together over the dark roads and sat waiting for the train for a long time. The platform was empty; theirs was the last train before the weekend. She handed him caramels to suck, and he felt her whole body tremble through the thigh he pressed hard against hers.

So much had built up in him while they waited that it was almost a relief when the train came sighing into the station. His mother stood and reached for Jude. He smiled up into her soft answering smile.

Then Jude's father stepped into the lights and scooped him up. His body under Jude's was taut, and Jude was so surprised that the shout caught in his throat. His mother did not look at her husband or her son. She seemed a statue, thin and pale.

At last, when the conductor said, All aboard! she gave an awful strangled sound and rushed through the train's door. The train hooted and slowly moved off. Jude could now shout, and did, as loudly as he could, although his father held him too firmly to escape, but the train vanished his mother into the darkness without stopping.

———

Then they were alone, Jude's father and he, in the house by the swamp.

Language wilted between them. Jude was the one who took up the sweeping and scrubbing, who made their sandwiches for supper. When his father was gone, he'd open the windows to let out some of the reptile rot. His father ripped up his mother's lilies and roses and planted mandarins and blueberries, saying that fruit brought birds and birds brought snakes. The boy walked three miles to school, where he told nobody that he already knew numbers better than the teachers did. He was small, but no one messed with him. On his first day, when a big ten-year-old tried to sneer at his clothes, Jude leapt at him with a viciousness he'd learned from watching rattlesnakes, and made the big boy's head bleed. The others avoided him. He was an in-between creature, motherless but not fatherless, stunted and ratty like a poor boy, but a professor's son, always correct with answers when the teachers called on him, but never offering a word on his own. The others kept their distance. Jude played by himself or with one of the succession of puppies that his father brought home. Inevitably, the dogs would run down to the edge of the swamp, and one of the fourteen- or fifteen-foot alligators would get them.

Jude's loneliness grew, became a living creature that

shadowed him and wandered off only when he was in the company of his numbers. More than marbles or tin soldiers, they were his playthings. More than sticks of candy or plums, they made his mouth water. As messy as the world was, the numbers, predictable and polite, brought order.

When he was ten, a short, round man stopped him on the street and pushed a brown-paper package into his arms. Jude found him vaguely familiar but couldn't place him. The man pressed a finger to his lips, minced away. At home in his room at night, Jude unwrapped the books. One was a collection of Frost's poems. The other was a book of geometry, the world whittled down until it became a series of lines and angles. He looked up and morning was sunshot through the laurel oaks. More than the feeling that the book had taught him geometry was the feeling that it had showed the boy something that had been living inside him, undetected until now.

There was also a letter. It was addressed to him in his mother's round hand. When he sat in school dividing the hours until he could be free, when he made the supper of tuna sandwiches, when he ate with his father, who conducted to Benny Goodman on the radio, when he brushed his teeth and put on pajamas far too small for him, the four perfect right angles of the letter called to him. He put it under his pillow, unopened. For a week, the letter burned under everything, the way the sun on a hot, overcast day was hidden but always present.

At last, having squeezed everything to know out of the geometry book, he put the still-sealed envelope inside and taped up the covers and hid it between his mattress and box spring. He checked it every night after saying his prayers and was comforted into sleep. When, one night, he saw the book was untaped and the letter gone, he knew his father had found it and nothing could be done.

The next time he saw the little round man on the street, he stopped him. Who are you? he asked, and the man blinked and said, Your uncle. When no comprehension passed over the boy's face, the man threw his arms up and said, Oh, honey! and made as if to hug him, but Jude had already turned away.

Inexorably, the university grew. It swelled and expanded under a steady supply of conditioned air, swallowing the land between it and the swamp until the university's roads were built snug against his father's land. Dinners, now, were full of his father's invective: Did the university not know that his snakes needed a home, that this expanse of sandy acres was one of the richest reptile havens in North America? He would never sell, never. He would kill to keep it.

While his father spoke, the traitor in Jude dreamed of

the sums his father had been offered. So simple, it seemed, to make the money grow. Unlike other kinds of numbers, money was already self-fertilized; it would double and double again until at last it made a roiling mass. If you had enough of it, Jude knew, nobody would ever have to worry again.

When Jude was thirteen, he discovered the university library. One summer day, he looked up from the pile of books he'd been contentedly digging through—trigonometry, statistics, calculus, whatever he could find—to see his father opposite him. Jude didn't know how long he'd been there. It was a humid morning, and even in the library the air was stifling, but his father looked leathered, cool in his sun-beaten shirt and red neckerchief.

Come on, then, he said. Jude followed, feeling ill. They rode in the pickup for two hours before Jude understood that they were going snaking together. This was his first time. When he was smaller, he'd begged to go, but every time, his father had said no, it was too dangerous, and Jude never argued that letting a boy live for a week alone in a house full of venom and guns and questionable wiring was equally unsafe.

His father pitched the tent and they ate beans from a can in the darkness. They lay side by side in their sleeping bags until his father said, You're good at math.

Jude said, I am, though with such understatement that it felt like a lie. Something shifted between them, and they fell asleep to a silence that was softer at its edges.

His father woke Jude before dawn and he stumbled out of the tent to grainy coffee with condensed milk and hot hush puppies. His father was after moccasins, and he gave Jude his waders and trudged through the swamp protected only by jeans and boots. He'd been bitten so often, he said, it had become routine. When he handed his son the stick and gestured at a black slash sunning on a rock, the boy had to imagine the snake as a line in space, only connecting point to point, to be able to grasp it. The snake spun from the number one to the number three to a defeated eight, and he deposited it in the sack. They worked in silence, only the noise of exuberant natural Florida filling their ears, the unafraid birds, the seethe of insects.

When Jude climbed back up into the truck at the end of the day, his legs shook from the effort it took him to be brave. So now you know, his father said in a strange, holy voice, and Jude was too tired to take the steps necessary then, and ever afterward until he was his father's own age, to understand.

His father began storing the fodder mice in Jude's closet, and to avoid the doomed squeaks, Jude joined the high school track team. He found his talent in the two-hundred-twenty-yard hurdles. When he came home with a trophy from the state games, his father held the trophy for a moment, then put it down.

Different if Negroes were allowed to run, he said.

Jude said nothing, and his father said, Lord knows I'm no lover of the race, but your average Negro could out-run any white boy I know.

Jude again said nothing, but avoided his father and didn't make him an extra steak when he cooked himself dinner. He still wasn't talking to him when his father went on an overnight trip and didn't come back for a week. Jude was used to it, and didn't get alarmed until the money ran out and his father still hadn't come home.

He alerted the secretary at the university, who sent out a group of graduate students to where Jude's father had been seen. They found the old man in his tent, bloated, his tongue protruding from a face turned black; and Jude understood then how even the things you loved most could kill you. He stored this knowledge in his bones and thought of it with every decision he made from then on.

At the funeral, out of a twisted loyalty to his father, he avoided his uncle. He didn't know if his mother knew she'd been widowed; he thought probably not. He told nobody at school that his father had died. He thought of himself as an island in the middle of the ocean, with no hope of seeing another island in the distance, or even a ship passing by.

Jude lived alone in the house. He let the mice die, then tossed the snakes in high twisting parabolas into the swamp. He scrubbed the house until it gleamed and the stench of reptiles was gone, then applied beeswax, paint, polish until it was a house fit for his mother. He waited. She didn't come.

The day he graduated from high school, Jude packed his clothes and sealed up the house and took the train to Boston. He'd heard from his uncle that his mother lived there, and so he'd applied and been accepted to college in the city. She owned a bookstore on a small, dark street. It took Jude a month of slow passing to gather the courage to go in. She was either in the back, or shelving books, or smiling in conversation with somebody, and he'd have a swim of darkness in his gut and know that it was fate telling him that today was not the day. When he went in, it was only because she was alone at the register, and her face—pouchy, waxy—was so sad in repose that the sight of it washed all thought from his head.

She rose with a wordless cry and flew to him. He held her stoically. She smelled like cats, and her clothes flopped on her as if she'd lost a lot of weight quickly. He told her about his father dying, and she nodded and said, I know, honey, I dreamed it.

She wouldn't let him leave her. She dragged him home with her and made him spaghetti carbonara and put clean sheets on the couch for him. Her three cats yowled under the door to her bedroom until she came back in with them. In the middle of the night, he woke to find her in her easy chair, clutching her hands, staring at him with glittering eyes. He closed his own and squeezed his hands into fists. He lay stiffly, almost shouting with the agony of being watched.

He went to see her once a week but refused all dinner invitations. He couldn't bear the density or lateness of her love. He was in his junior year when her long-percolating illness overcame her and she, too, left him. Now he was alone.

There was nothing but numbers then.

Later, there would be numbers but also the great ravishing machine in the laboratory into which Jude fed punched slips of paper and the motorcycle he rode because it roared like murder. He had been given a class to teach, but it was taken away after a month and he was told that he was better suited for research. In his late twenties, there were drunk and silly girls he could seduce without saying a word, because they felt a kind of danger coiled in him.

He rode his motorcycle too fast over icy roads. He swam at night in bays where great whites had been spotted. He bombed down ski slopes with only a hazy idea of the mechanics of snow. He drank so many beers he woke one morning to discover he'd developed a paunch as big as a pregnant woman's belly. He laughed to shake it, liked its wobble. It felt comforting, a child's pillow clutched to his midsection all day long.

By the time he was thirty, Jude was weary. He became drawn to bridges, their tensile strength, the cold river flowing underneath. A resolution was forming under his thoughts, like a contusion hardening under the skin.

And then he was crossing a road, and he hadn't looked first, and a bread truck, filled with soft dinner rolls so yeasty and warm that they were still expanding in their trays, hit him. He woke with a leg twisted beyond recognition, a mouth absent of teeth on one side, and his head in the lap of a woman who was crying for him, though she was a stranger, and he was bleeding all over her skirt, and there were warm mounds of bread scattered around them. It was the bread that made the pain return to his body, the deep warmth and good smell. He bit the hem of the woman's skirt to keep from screaming.

She rode with him to the hospital and stayed all night to keep him from falling asleep and possibly going into a coma. She was homely, three years older than he, a thick-legged antiques dealer who described her shop down a street so tiny the sun never touched her windows. He thought of her in the silent murky shop, swimming from credenza to credenza. She fed him rice pudding when she came to visit him in the hospital, and carefully brushed his wild hair until it was flat on his crown.

One night he woke with a jerk: the stars were angrily bright in the hospital window and someone in the room was breathing. There was a weight on his chest, and when he looked down, he found the woman's sleeping head. For a moment, he didn't know who she was. By the time he identified her, the feeling of unknowing had burrowed in. He would never know her; knowledge of another person was ungraspable, a cloud. He would never begin to hold another in his mind like an equation, pure and entire. He focused on the part of her thin hair, which in the darkness and closeness looked like inept stitches in white wax. He stared at the part until the horror faded, until her smell, the bitterness of unwashed hair, the lavender soap she used on her face, rose to him, and he put his nose against her warmth and inhaled her.

At dawn, she woke. Her cheek was creased from the folds in his gown. She looked at him wildly and he laughed, and she rubbed the drool from the corner of her mouth and turned away as if disappointed. He married her because to not do so had ceased to be an option during the night.

While he was learning how to walk again, he had a letter from the university down in Florida that made a tremendous offer for his father's land.

And so, instead of the honeymoon trip to the Thousand Islands, pines and cold water and his wife's bikini pressing into the dough of her flesh, they took a sleeping train down to Florida and walked in the heat to the edge of the university campus. Where he remembered vast oak hummocks, there were rectilinear brick buildings. Mossy pools were now parking lots.

Only his father's property, one hundred acres, was overgrown with palmettos and vines. He brushed the red bugs off his wife's sensible travel pants and carried her into his father's house. Termites had chiseled long gouges in the floorboards, but the sturdy Cracker house had kept out most of the wilderness. His wife touched the mantel made of heart pine and turned to him gladly. Later, after he came home with a box of groceries and found the kitchen scrubbed clean, he heard three thumps upstairs and ran up to find that she had killed a black snake in the bathtub with her bare heel and was laughing at herself in amazement.

How magnificent he found her, a Valkyrie, half naked and warlike with that dead snake at her feet. In her body, the culmination of all things. He didn't say it, of course; he couldn't. He only reached and put his hands upon her.

In the night, she rolled toward him and took his ankles between her own. All right, she said. We can stay.

I didn't say anything, he said.

And she smiled a little bitterly and said, Well. You don't.

They moved their things into the house where he was born. They put in air-conditioning, renovated the structure, put on large additions. His wife opened a shop and drove to Miami and Atlanta to stock it with antiques. He sold his father's land, but slowly, in small pieces, at prices that rose dizzyingly with each sale. The numbers lived in him, warmed him, brought him a buzzing kind of joy. Jude made investments so shrewd that when he and his wife were in their mid-thirties, he opened a bottle of wine and announced that neither of them would ever have to work again. His wife laughed and drank but kept up with the store. When she was almost too old, they had a daughter and named her after his mother.

When he held the baby at home for the first time, he understood he had never been so terrified of anything as he was of this mottled lump of flesh. How easily he could break her without meaning to. She could slip from his hands and crack open on the floor; she could catch pneumonia when he bathed her; he could say a terrible thing in anger and she would shrivel. All the mistakes he could make telescoped before him. His wife saw him turn pale and plucked the baby from his hands just before he crashed down. When he came to, she was livid but calm. He protested, but she put the baby in his hands.

Try again, she said.

His daughter grew, sturdy and blonde like his wife, with no ash of Jude's genius for numbers. They were as dry as biscuits in her mouth; she preferred music and English. For this, he was glad. She would love more moderately, more externally. If he didn't cuddle with her the way her mother did, he still thought he was a good father: he never hit her, he never left her alone in the house, he told her how much he loved her by providing her with everything he could imagine she'd like. He was a quiet parent, but he was sure she knew the scope of his heart.

And yet his daughter never grew out of wearing a singularly irritating expression, one taut with competition, which she first wore when she was a very little girl at an Easter egg hunt. She could barely walk in her grass-stained bloomers, but even when the other children rested out of the Florida sunshine in the shade, eating their booty of chocolate, Jude's little girl kept returning with eggs too cunningly hidden in the sago palms to have been found in the first frenzy. She heaped them on his lap until they overflowed, and she shrieked when he told her firmly that enough was enough.

His fat old uncle came over for dinner once, then once a week, then became a friend. When the uncle died of an aneurysm while feeding his canary, he left Jude his estate of moth-eaten smoking jackets and family photos in ornate frames.

The university grew around Jude's last ten-acre parcel, a protective cushion between the old house and the rest of the world. The more construction around their plot of land, the fewer snakes Jude saw, until he felt no qualms about walking barefoot in the St. Augustine grass to take the garbage to the edge of the drive. He built a fence around his land and laughed at the university's offers, sensing desperation in their inflating numbers. He thought of himself as the virus in the busy cell, latent, patient. The swamp's streams were blocked by the university's construction, and it became a small lake, in which he installed some bubblers to keep the mosquitoes away. There were alligators, sometimes large ones, but he put in an invisible fence, and it kept his family's dogs from coming too close to the water's edge and being gobbled up. The gators only eyed them from the banks.

And then, one day, Jude woke with the feeling that a bell jar had descended over him. He showered with a sense of unease, sat at the edge of the bed for a while. When his wife came in to tell him something, he watched in confusion at the way her mouth opened and closed fishily, without sound.

I think I've gone deaf, he said, and he didn't so much hear his words as feel them vibrating in the bones of his skull.

At the doctor's, he submitted to test after test, but nobody understood what had gone wrong in his brain or in his ears. They gave him a hearing aid that turned conversation into an underwater burble. Mostly, he kept it off.

At night, he'd come out into the dark kitchen, longing for curried chicken, raw onion, preserved peaches, tastes sharp and simple to remind himself that he was still there. He'd find his daughter at the kitchen island, her lovely mean face lit up by her screen. She'd frown at him and turn the screen to show him what she'd discovered: cochlear implants, audiologic rehabilitation, miracles.

But there was nothing for him. He was condemned. He ate Thanksgiving dinner wanting to weep into his sweet potatoes. His family was gathered around him, his wife and daughter and their closest friends and their children, and he could see them laughing, but he couldn't hear the jokes. He longed for someone to look up, to see him at the end of the table, to reach out a hand and pat his. But they were too happy. They slotted full forks into their mouths and brought the tines out clean. They picked the flesh off the turkey, they scooped the pecans out of the pie.

After the dinner, his arms prickling with hot water from the dishes, they sat together watching football, and he lay back in his chair with his feet propped up, and all of the children fell asleep around him on the couch, and he alone sat in vigil over them, watching them sleep.

The day his daughter went to college in Boston, his wife went with her.

She mouthed very carefully to him, You'll be all right for four days? You can take care of yourself?

And he said, Yes, of course. I am an *adult*, sweetheart, but the way she winced, he knew he'd said it too loudly. He loaded their bags into the car, and his daughter cried in his arms, and he kissed her over and over on the crown of the head. His wife looked at him worriedly but kissed him also and climbed inside. And then, silently as everything, the car moved off.

The house felt immense around him. He sat in the study, which had been his childhood bedroom, and seemed to see the place as it had been, spare and filled with snakes, layered atop the house as it was, with its marble and bright walls and track lights above his head.

That night, he waited, his hearing aid turned up so loudly that it began to make sharp beeping sounds that hurt. He wanted the pain. He fell asleep watching a sitcom that, without sound, was just strange-looking people making huge expressions with their faces, and he woke up and it was only eight o'clock at night, and he felt as if he'd been alone forever.

He hadn't known he'd miss his wife's heavy body in the bed next to his, the sandwiches she made (too much mayonnaise, but he never told her so), the smell of her body wash in the humid bathroom in the morning.

On the second night, he sat in the black density of the veranda, looking at the lake that used to be a swamp. He wondered what had happened to the reptiles out there, where they had gone. Alone in the darkness, Jude wished he could hear the university in its nighttime boil around him, the students shouting drunkenly, the bass thrumming, the noise of football games out at the stadium that used to make Jude and his wife groan with irritation. But he could have been anywhere, in the middle of hundreds of miles of wasteland, as quiet as the night was for him. Even the mosquitoes had somehow diminished. As a child, he would have been a single itchy blister by now.

Unable to sleep, Jude climbed to the roof to straighten the gutter that had crimped in the middle from a falling oak branch. He crept on his hands and knees across the asbestos shingles, still hot from the day, to fix the flashing on the chimney. From up there, the university coiled around him, and in the streetlights, a file of pledging sorority girls in tight, bright dresses and high heels slowly crawled up the hill like ants.

He came down reluctantly at dawn and took a can of tuna and a cold jug of water down to the lake's edge, where he turned over the aluminum johnboat his wife had bought for him a few years earlier, hoping he'd take up fishing.

Fishing? he'd said, I haven't fished since I was a boy. He thought of those childhood shad and gar and snook, how his father cooked them up with the lemons from the tree beside the back door and ate them without a word of praise. He must have made a face because his wife had recoiled.

I thought it'd be a hobby, she'd said. If you don't like it, find another hobby. Or *something*.

He'd thanked her but had never had the time to use either the rod or the boat. It sat there, its bright belly dulling under layers of pollen. Now was the time. He was hungry for something indefinable, something he thought he'd left behind him so long ago. He thought he might find it in the lake, perhaps.

He pushed off and rowed out. There was no wind, and the sun was already searing. The water was hot and thick with algae. A heron stood one-legged among the cypress. Something big jumped and sent rings out toward the boat, rocking it slightly. Jude tried to get comfortable but was sweating, and now the mosquitoes smelled him and swarmed. The silence was eerie because he remembered the lake as a dense tapestry of sound, the click and whirr of the sandhill cranes, the cicadas, the owls, the mysterious subhuman cries too distant to identify. He had wanted to connect with something, something he had lost, but it wasn't here.

He gave up. But when he sat up to row himself back, both oars had slid loose from their locks and floated off. They lay ten feet away, caught in the duckweed.

The water thickly hid its danger, but he knew what was there. There were the alligators, their knobby eyes even now watching him. He'd seen one with his binoculars from the bedroom the other day that was at least fourteen feet long. He felt it somewhere nearby now. And though this was no longer prairie, there were still a few snakes, cottonmouths, copperheads, pygmies under the leaf rot at the edge of the lake. There was the water itself, superheated until it hosted flagellates that enter the nose and infect the brain, an infinity of the minuscule eating away. There was the burning sun above and the mosquitoes feeding on his blood. There was the silence. He wouldn't swim in this terrifying mess. He stood, agitated, and felt the boat slide a few inches from under him, and he sat down hard, clinging to the gunwales. He was a hundred feet offshore on a breathless day. He would not be blown to shore. He would be stuck here forever; his wife would come home in two days to find his corpse floating in its johnboat. He drank some water to calm himself. When he decided to remember algorithms in his head, their savor had stolen away.

For now, there were silent birds and sun and mosquitoes; below, a world of slinking predators. In the delicate cup of the johnboat, he was alone. He closed his eyes and felt his heart beat in his ears.

He had never had the time to be seized by doubt. Now all he had was time. Hours dripped past. He sweated. He was ill. The sun only grew hotter, and there was no respite, no shade.

Jude drifted off to sleep, and when he woke, he knew that if he opened his eyes, he would see his father sitting in the bow, glowering. Terrible son, Jude was, to ruin what his father loved best. The ancient fear rose in him, and he swallowed it as well as he could with his dry throat. He would not open his eyes, he wouldn't give the old man the satisfaction.

Go away, he said. Leave me be. His voice inside his head was only a rumble.

His father waited, patient and silent, a dark dense mass at the end of the boat.

I'm not like you, Dad, Jude said later. I don't prefer snakes to people.

The sun pushed down; the smell on the air was his father's smell. Jude breathed from his mouth.

Even later, he said, You were a nasty, unhappy man. And I always hated you.

But this seemed harsh, and he said, I didn't completely mean that.

He thought of this lake. He thought of how his father would see Jude's life. Such a delicate ecosystem, so precisely calibrated, in the end destroyed by Jude's careful parceling of love, of land. Greed, the university's gobble. Those scaled creatures, killed. The awe in his father's voice that day they went out gathering moccasins; the bright, sharp love inside Jude, long ago, when he had loved numbers. Jude's promise was unfulfilled, the choices made not the passionate ones. Jude had been safe.

And still, here he was. Alone as his father was when he died in that tent. Isolated. Sunbattered. Old.

He thought in despair of diving into the perilous water, and how he probably deserved being bitten. But then the wind picked up and began pushing him back across the lake, toward his house. When he opened his eyes, his father wasn't with him, but the house loomed over the bow, ramshackle, too huge, a crazy person's place. He averted his eyes, unable to bear it now. The sun snuffed itself out. Despite his pain, the skin on his legs and arms blistered with sunburn and great, itching mosquito welts, he later realized he must have fallen asleep because, when he opened his eyes again, the stars were out and the john-boat was nosing up against the shore.

He stood, his bones aching, and wobbled to the shore.

And now something white and large was rushing at him, and because he'd sat all day with his father's ghost, he understood this was a ghost, too, and looked up at it, calm and ready. The lights from the house shined at its back, and it had a golden glow around it. But the figure stopped just before him, and he saw, with a startle, that it was his wife, that the glow was her frizzy gray hair catching the light, and he knew then that she must have come back early, that she was reaching a hand out to him, putting her soft palm on his cheek, and she was saying something forever lost to him, but he knew by the way she was smiling that she was scolding him. He stepped closer to her and put his head in the crook of her neck and breathed his inadequacy out there, breathed in her love and the grease of her travels and knew he had been lucky, and that he had escaped the hungry dark once more.

DOGS GO WOLF

The storm came and erased the quiet.

Well, the older sister thought, an island is never really quiet. Even without the storm, there were waves and wind and air conditioners and generators and animals moving out there in the dark.

What the storm had erased was the silence from the other cabin. For hours, there had been no laughing, no bottle caps falling, none of the bickering that the girls had grown used to over the past two days.

This was because there were no more adults. They'd been left alone on the island, the two little girls. Four and seven. Pretty little things, strangers called them. What dolls! Their faces were exactly like their mother's. Hoochies in waiting, their mother joked, but she watched them anxiously from the corner of her eye. She was a good mother.

The fluffy white dog had at least stopped his yowling. He had crept close to the girls' bed, but when they tried to stroke him, he snapped at their hands. The animal was

torn between his hatred of children and his hatred of the
wild storm outside.

The big sister said, Once upon a time, there was a—
—princess, the little sister said.

Rabbit, the big sister said.

Rabbit princess, the little sister said.

Once upon a time, there was a tiny purple rabbit, the
older sister said. A man saw her and scooped her up in his
net. Her family tried to stop him, but they couldn't. The
man went into the city and took the rabbit to a pet store
and put her into a box in the window. All day long people
stuck their hands in to touch the purple rabbit. Finally, a
girl came in and bought the rabbit and took her home. It
was better there, but the rabbit still missed her family. She
grew and slept with the girl in her bed, but most days she
stared out the window all sad. She began to forget that
she was a rabbit. One day, the girl put a leash on the rabbit
and they went out into the park. The rabbit looked up
and saw another rabbit staring at her from the edge of the
woods. They looked at each other long enough for her
to remember that she was not a girl but a rabbit, and the
other rabbit was her own sister. The girl was kind to her
and gave her food, but the rabbit looked at her sister and
she knew that this was her only chance. She slipped out
of the collar and ran as fast as she could over the field,
and she and her sister hopped into the forest. The rabbit

family was so happy to see her. They had a party, dancing and singing and eating cabbage and carrots. The end.

The little sister was asleep. The two fishing cabins rocked on their stilts, the dock ground against the shore, the wind spoke through the cracks in the window frames, the palms lashed, the waves shattered and roared. The older girl held her little sister.

All night, she and the island were awake, the island because it never slept, the girl because she knew that only her ferocious attention would keep them safe.

Before they were left alone in the fishing camp on the island in the middle of the ocean, there had been Smokey Joe and Melanie. They were strangers to the girls. He wore a red bandanna above his eyebrows. Her shirts couldn't hold in all her flesh.

The older girl knew that the two adults were nervous, because they didn't stop smoking and arguing in hushed voices while the girls watched *Snow White* over and over. It was the only tape they'd brought. In the afternoon, Smokey Joe took the girls on a walk to the pond at the center of the island. It was a weird place. Beyond the sandy bay where the dock and the cabin were, the land grew rough with a kind of spongy stone and the trees seemed shrunken and bent by the wind.

Watch out, he told them. A Hollywood movie had been made here a long time ago and some monkeys had escaped. You come close, they'll rip your hair out and steal your food from your bowl and throw poop at your head. He was joking, maybe. It was hard to tell.

They didn't see any monkeys, though they did see huge black palmetto bugs, a rat snake sunning itself on the sandy path, long-necked white birds that Smokey Joe called ibises.

In the cabin, Melanie gave them hamburger patties without ketchup or buns and told them not to touch the dog because he was a mean little sucker. The younger sister didn't listen, and suddenly her forearm was bleeding. Melanie shrugged and said, Told you. The older girl got one of their mother's maxi pads from her dopp kit and wrapped it, sticker side out, around her sister's arm.

Smokey Joe sat outside all afternoon under the purple tree with its nubby green banana fingers. He was listening to his CB radio. Then he stood up and shouted for Melanie. Melanie ran out, her breasts and belly moving in all kinds of directions under her shirt. The older sister heard Smokey Joe say, Safer to leave 'em.

Melanie poked her head into the cabin. She was pale under her orangey tan.

She said, Stay here. If someone shows up, don't you go with no man. Girls, listen to me. Stay here, be good. I'll send a lady to get you in a few hours.

The girls went outside and watched Smokey Joe and Melanie running down the dock. Melanie was screaming for the dog, but the dog stood still and didn't follow her.

LAUREN GROFF

And then Joe threw off the lines and Melanie jumped
into the boat, almost missing it. One leg dangled in the
water, then she lifted it over the side and they took off at
full speed.

Before that, exactly one day before Smokey Joe and
Melanie left the girls alone on the island, their mother
had come to them in their own cabin, and she was dressed
all fancy and smelled like a garden. Her boyfriend Ernesto and she were going out in Ernesto's boat, she said.
We'll only be gone for an hour or two, honey bears. She
pressed them close to her, her face made up with blue
eyeshadow, her eyelashes so thick and long that it was a
wonder she could see. She left red kisses on their cheeks.

But the hours clicked by and she didn't come back at
all. When night fell, the girls had to sleep on the floor in
Melanie and Smokey Joe's cabin, and Melanie and Smokey
Joe whispered behind their bedroom door all night.

And, two days before that, their mother had come
into the girls' room in Fort Lauderdale in the middle of
the night and thrown a few of their things into a bag and
said, We're going on a boat ride, pretties! Ernesto's going
to make us rich, and she laughed. Their mother was so
beautiful she just glinted off light. Before the sun was
even up, they were on Ernesto's boat, going fast through
the dark. And then they'd come to this little island, and
the adults had talked all day and all night in the other
cabin, and their mother had seemed wild on the inside,
flushed on the outside.

48

And before Ernesto, many nights before him, their mother would come home very late, jangling. She usually made dinner for the girls, then left the older girl in charge of getting her sister's teeth brushed and reading her to sleep. The older girl never slept in her own bed, always just stayed beside her sister until their mother was home. Sometimes, when the mother came in, she would get the girls up in their nightgowns, the night still in the windows, and sprinklers spitting in the courtyard, and she'd smell of vodka and smoke and money, and would put music on too loud and they'd all dance. Their mother would smoke cigarettes and fry up eggs and pancakes that she'd top with strawberry ice cream. She'd talk about the other women she worked with: idiots, she called them. Skanks. She didn't trust other women. They were all backstabbing bitches who'd rob you sooner than help you. She liked men. Men were easy. You knew where you were with men. Women were too complicated. You always had to guess. You couldn't give them an inch or they'd ruin you, she said.

Before they came to Fort Lauderdale's blazing sun, they had been in Traverse City, where the older girl remembered only cherries and frozen fingers.

Before Traverse City, San Jose with its huge aloe plants and the laundromat below their apartment chugging all day.

Before San Jose, Brookline, where the little sister came to them in a tiny blanket of blue and pink stripes, a cocked hat.

Before Brookline, Phoenix, where they lived with a man who may have been the little sister's father.

Before Phoenix, she was too small to remember. Or maybe there was nothing.

The morning was painfully clear. Once, at Goodwill, the mother had found a glass that she rang with a fingernail, and the glass sang in a high and perfect voice. The sunlight was like that after the storm.

There was nobody to tell them not to, so they ate grape jelly with spoons for breakfast. They watched *Snow White* on the VCR again.

The dog whimpered at the door. He had a little pad in the bathroom where he did his business. Melanie's so damn lazy, their mother had muttered when she first saw the pad. What a lazy bitch. But maybe, the older sister thought, the dog just needed a little air. She got up and put his pink leash on and let him out. The dog went down the steps so fast that he pulled the leash out of her hand. He looked back at the girl, and she could see the gears turning in his head, then he sped off into the woods. She called for him, but he wouldn't come.

She went inside and didn't tell her sister what had happened. It wasn't until dinner—tuna fish and crackers and cheese—that the little sister looked around and said, Where's the dog?

The older sister shrugged and said, I think he ran off.

The little sister started crying, and both girls went outside with a bowl of water and a can of tuna and opened it and called and called for the dog. He trotted out of the forest. There were sticks in his fur and mud on his belly, but he looked happy. He wouldn't come near the girls, only growled until they went inside and then watched them through the screen door as he gulped down his food. The older sister lunged out the door and tried to grab his leash, but he was too fast and disappeared again.

The little girl stopped crying only when her sister brought out Melanie's cookies. Don't you touch my damn Oreos, she'd said to them, but she wasn't around to yell now. They ate them all.

Late at night, there was a terrible grinding sound, and the girls went outside with flashlights and looked at the air-conditioning unit and saw that a brown snake had fallen into it from the palm trees; with every turn of the blade, a millimeter more of the snake was being eaten by the fan. They watched the snake dissolve bit by bit until the skin fell all the way through and lay, empty of meat, on the ground.

The girls woke up sticky and hot. The air-conditioning had died sometime before dawn.

The older one thought the snake had gummed things

up, but nothing was working—no lights, no water pump, no refrigerator—and then she understood that it was the generator. She went out back and kicked it. She found a hole where the gas went in and looked inside with her flashlight.

We runned out of gas, she told her sister, who was sucking her fingers again, the way she had when she was a baby.

Fix it, the little sister said, I'm so hot. But they looked and looked, and there was no more fuel. When the older sister tried to flush the toilet, it wouldn't flush. When the cabin started to smell from the toilet and the dog's pad, they moved back to the other cabin, where their mother's stuff was still in the closets and on the dresser. They began going to the bathroom outside.

There was no food in their cabin, so they took everything they could find from Melanie and Smokey Joe's. Frozen peas, which they ate like popcorn, one Hungry-Man TV dinner, which they opened and left out for the dog. A block of cheese and yellow mustard. White bread, more cheese in a spray can, a can of beans. Bourbon and cigars that smelled like a spice drawer.

In the afternoon, they put on their mother's clothes, her makeup. They looked like tiny versions of her, both of them, though the little sister didn't need to go in the sun to be tanned.

The older sister read everything she could to her little sister. There was one fat book, yellow and swollen, on

Melanie's nightstand. It had a man on the cover with an axe over his shoulder but no shirt. She read the cereal box she dug out of the garbage. She read the old magazines on the coffee table.

The older girl understood that there was no more water only when they were thirsty and she tried to turn on the faucet. She ignored her thirst for a long time, until her throat felt stuffed with cotton and the little girl wouldn't stop complaining.

It was going to be dark in a half hour or so. The sun was burning at the edge of the ocean.

The older sister sighed. I think we have to walk to the pond, she said.

The little sister started to cry. But the monkeys, she said.

We'll make lots of noise. They won't bother us if we're together, the older sister said, and they walked very fast, hand in hand, to the pond, and it was twilight when they got back. The girls saw a white flash in the woods, and the little one was so frightened that she dropped her bucket and spilled half her water, and she ran all the way back to the cabin, slamming the door. The older sister cried with rage and carried the buckets back by herself. Out of meanness, she wouldn't let her little sister drink the water until she'd put it in a saucepan and set it over the charcoal grill to boil, which took a very, very long time, until the moon was fat and bright in the sky.

n the morning, the older girl took out her sister's braids and the little one's hair fluffed out into a beautiful dark cloud.

They took the only knife, a steak knife, and whittled points into the ends of sticks, and they went into the chilly shallow water to fish, because they'd have to find food soon. But the water was so nice and the fish were so little that they abandoned the spears and swam all morning.

They painted their fingernails with polish they found in Melanie's medicine cabinet. Then they painted their toenails, then tattoos of hearts on their biceps, which made their skin itch until they scratched the hearts off.

They found a candy bar in a nightstand, then a dirty magazine under Smokey Joe's bed. A woman was licking a pearl off another woman's pink private skin.

Yuck, the older sister said, and threw the magazine, but the younger sister made the noises the mother made when she was in her bedroom with her boyfriends. Then she started crying. At first, she only shook her head when her sister asked her why. Finally she said, I miss the dog.

Nobody could miss that dog, the older sister thought.

How could Melanie leave him? the little sister said.

Then the older sister thought, Oh.

Let's go on a dog hunt, she said.

They took the steak knife, binoculars, an old whiskey

bottle with the last of their boiled water, and a giant panama hat they'd found in a closet, which the older sister wore because she burned to blisters all the time. They took the rest of the crackers and sprayed themselves with the last of Melanie's Skin So Soft bug spray.

The little sister was happy again. It was early afternoon. There was no wind, and the heat of the clearing cooled when they went into the forest. They sang the dog's name, walking. The older sister nervously scanned the branches for monkeys.

The pond held a great gray heron, unmoving, like a sculpture. There were cypress knees, like stalagmites, in the shallows.

On the far side of the pond, there was a small wooden rowboat turned upside down. It was a flaking blue. The older sister kicked it, wondering how to drag it through the forest toward the cove and the dock. Then she wondered how she would make sure, once they'd launched it, that they floated toward land and not into the deep-blue sea. Maybe it was best just to wait for the lady Melanie was supposed to send.

When she looked up, her little sister had vanished. Her heart dropped out of her body. She called her sister's name, then screamed it over and over.

She heard a laugh from below, and her sister slid out from under a lip of rock that made a shallow invisible cave. That was so mean, the older sister yelled, and the little sister shrugged and said, Sorry, though she wasn't.

There could've been snakes there, the older sister said.

But there weren't, the little one said.

They walked all the way across the island and found a yellow sand beach on the other side. Their dresses were soaked with sweat when they got back to the pond and filled the whiskey bottle up with green water.

Back in the fishing camp, the dog was waiting on the steps. The girls poured out unboiled water for him, and the dog lapped it up, watching them with his angry black-button eyes. Even though the little sister sang softly to him in her voice that their mother always said would knock the angels out of heaven, the dog wouldn't come near, and backed into the forest again.

The girls' clothes were so dirty that they put on Smokey Joe's last two clean T-shirts. They swept the path behind the girls like ball gowns when they ran, flashes of red and blue through the green-gold forest.

The little sister carried her bucket all the way back from the pond without complaining.

They caught three crabs under the dock with their hands and boiled them, and the flesh tasted like butter, and the water they boiled the crabs in they drank like soup, and afterward they felt full for a little while.

Then the rest of the food was gone. The bananas on the tree, Smokey Joe had said, were not ripe yet and would make them sick if they tried to eat them. The older sister had heard of people eating bugs and there were plenty of cockroaches everywhere, but the thought of the crunch under her teeth made her feel ill.

They ate cherry ChapStick. They opened an unlabeled can they found in the back of the cabinet, mandarin oranges. They ate strange red berries from the bushes, though the mother had always said never to do that.

I'm hungry, the little sister said.

Once upon a time, the big sister said, there was a boy and a girl whose family had no food at all. You could see their ribs. The mother had a boyfriend who didn't like the kids. One day, the boyfriend told the mother that they had to get rid of the kids and that he was going to take them for a hike and leave them way out in the woods. The girl had heard the adults talking that night, and in the morning, she filled her pockets with cereal.

They weren't starving if they had cereal, the little sister said.

The girl filled her pockets with blue pebbles from the fish tank. And when the boyfriend led them out into the woods she dropped the pebbles one by one by the side of the path so that when he vanished they could find their way back. The boy and the girl followed the stones home, and the mother was so happy to see them. But the boyfriend grew angry. The next day, he took them out again, but he'd sewn up their pockets so they couldn't leave a trail. He left them, and they wandered and wandered and found a cave to hide in for the night. The next morning they smelled woodsmoke and followed it to find a little cabin out in the woods, made of cookies and candy. So they ran over and started taking bites out of the house because they hadn't eaten in a long time. A lady came out. She was nice to them, and she kept giving them cake and mini pizzas.

And milk, the younger sister said. And apples.

There was a television. The lady didn't even make them sit down to eat their food; they just lay there and watched cartoons and ate all day long. The boy and the girl got really fat. And when they were superfat, the lady tied them up and tried to shove them into the oven like turkeys. But the girl was smart. She said, Oh, let me give you one last kiss! And the lady leaned her head forward, and the girl took a bite out of her throat. Because she'd become a champion eater at the lady's house, she ate the lady all the way down until there was nothing left, not even blood. And the boy and the girl stayed all winter eating the cookie house, and when spring came, they'd turned into adults. Then they went to find the boyfriend.

Why? the little sister said.

To eat him, the older sister said.

People eat people? the little sister said.

Sometimes you just have to, the big sister said.

No, the little sister said.

Fine. The lady was made of whipped cream, then, the

older sister said. They never found the boyfriend. But they would have eaten him if they had.

The older sister's head was gentle with clouds. The sand of the bay smelled like almonds to her. She was sitting alone by the charcoal grill, waiting for the water to boil. Her sister was inside, singing herself to sleep. She was happy, the older sister realized. Overhead was the thinning moon. Across the water came the squeak and rattle of some big birds with blood-red throats that were passing on their way to somewhere colder, somewhere larger, somewhere better than here.

There's a man, the little sister said from the screen door. There's no man, the older sister said dreamily.

He's in a boat. On the dock, the little sister said, and now the big sister could hear the purr of the motor. She stood up so fast that her head lost blood and she fell and then got to her knees and stood again.

Go, she whispered, and dragged her sister through the door, down the steps, into the woods.

They crouched in the ferns, and the ferns covered them. They were naked, and the ground beneath their bare feet could have been full of snakes, lizards, spiders.

The man's boots pounded down the dock. He came into view. He was stocky, with jeans and a sweaty T-shirt, a thick gold chain around his neck. The older sister knew—something whispered silently to her—that he was, in fact, a bad man.

Be quiet, the whisper said. Get away.

He went into the girls' cabin and there were crashing noises; he went into Melanie and Smokey Joe's cabin and again there were crashing noises. When he came out, he kicked over the grill, and the older girl put her hand over her sister's mouth to keep her from crying out. He turned around slowly, looking into the woods.

Come on out, he shouted. He had an accent. I know you're here.

He waited and said, We got your mama with us. Don't you want to see your mama? We'll make you a big old feast, and you can sit in her lap and eat it all up. Bet you're hungry.

The older sister struggled to keep the little one from standing. The man must have heard, because his head swiveled in their direction.

Run, the older girl said, and they ran through the woods, the palmettos lashing at their ankles and making them bleed. They found the path, they found the pond.

The older girl slid into the cave near the boat, then her little sister came in, and she held her tightly.

Soon they heard the man's footsteps crashing and his breath wheezing in and out, hard. Girls, he said, I saw you. I know you're around here.

His boots came into view, so close. He moved toward

the boat and kicked it once, twice, then the girls saw the rotten wood break apart, and a hundred frightened bugs ran out.

Fine, he said. Ain't going to chase you all day. Starve to death if you like.

The girls were silent, shaking, until they heard his footsteps fading. After too long, they heard the boat start up, then the motor thinned and he was gone. Still, they waited.

There was a rustling at their feet, and the little dog slunk out of the cave, where he must have been hiding all this time, inches away. The girls watched him gather the pink leash in his mouth and trot himself off.

Where's the lady? the little sister said. She's taking a long time.

What lady? the older sister said.

The one to save us, the little sister said. That Melanie's sending.

The older sister had forgotten there was supposed to be a lady. The girls were deep in their nest. They'd taken all the pillows and sheets in the camp, and piled them in the middle of the living room of their cabin, where a breeze passed over their sweaty bodies on its way from the screen door out the window. It was late in the morning, but the girls' bones didn't want to get up. Lie still, the bones said. Their hearts made music in their ears.

The older sister could almost see the lady now, coming down the dock. She'd wear a blue dress with a skirt so huge they could hide beneath it; she'd have their mother's yellow hair that was dark at the roots. She'd smile down at them. Girls, she'd whisper. Come home with me.

They hadn't eaten in three days. Somewhere not too far away, the white dog had howled all night until his howls sounded like wind. The older sister had dreamed of the courtyard of their Fort Lauderdale apartment, of the fountain's turquoise water and the red-dyed cedar mulch and the tree heavy with sweet oranges that almost peeled themselves in your fingers, the golden sun pouring down over everything, all of it shimmering but untouchable, as if behind glass.

Night came, day came, night came.

The dog had gone silent. The little sister's ribs were sharp beneath her skin. Her eyes were hot, the way their mother's were hot when she came home from work, wanting to dance, smoke, sing.

The older sister's body was made of air. She was a balloon, skidding over the ground. The light on the waves in the bay made her cry, but not with sadness. It was so beautiful, it wanted to speak to her; it was about to say something if she only watched hard enough.

The zip of a mosquito near her ear was a needling

beauty. She let the mosquito land on her skin, and slowly it pulsed and pumped and she felt her blood rising up into the small creature.

It was all so much. Through the years to come, she'd remember these days of calm. She'd hold these beautiful soft days in her as the years slowly moved from terrible to bearable to better, and she would feel herself growing, sharpening. She'd learn the language of men and use it against them: she'd become a lawyer. Her little sister, so lovely, so fragile, only ever wanted to be held. For a long time, the older sister was the one who did this for her. She was the shell. But then the little sister met a man who first gave her love, then withdrew it until she believed the things he believed. He made her give up her last name, which the older sister had fought their whole childhood to keep, though their third foster parents had wanted to adopt them, because it was the only thing they had of their mother. And then one day the older sister stood in the pews and watched her baby sister get married to this man. She wore a white dress with a skirt so giant she could barely walk, and bound herself to that man. The older sister watched and started to shake. She cried. An ugly wish spread in her like ink in water: that she and her sister had stayed on the island all those years ago; that they'd slowly vanished into their hunger until they turned into sunlight and dust.

Once upon a time, the older sister croaked, and the little sister whispered, No. Shush, please.

Once upon a time, the older sister said, there were two little girls made out of air. They were so beautiful that everyone who saw them wanted to scoop them up and put them into their pockets. One day, the god of wind saw them and loved them so much that he lifted them up and took them with him to the clouds to be his daughters. And they lived there forever with their father, and it was full of rainbows and people singing and good things to eat and soft beds made of feathers.

The end, the little sister said.

The younger sister dozed in the cabin. The older one let her body float above the path to the pond and back with water. There was no more charcoal, so they had to boil it over sticks she'd collected on the way back.

Twenty feet from the cabins, she heard the slightest of sounds. She peered into the palmettos and saw a glint of metal. She walked through the prickles and not one reached out to scratch her.

It was the dog. He had spun his leash so tightly around a scrub oak that his tongue was extended and his eyes bulged. He was no longer white fluff but knots of yellow and brown string.

The girl took the steak knife from her belt and knelt and sawed and sawed. She had to take breaks, because she kept getting dizzy. At last the leash broke and the dog stood and stumbled off into the underbrush again. There he would live forever, the girl knew. He would stay in that forest, running and howling and eating birds and fish and lizards. That dog was too mean to ever die.

She came back to find her sister naked outside the cabin, under the banana tree. Look, the little girl said dreamily, sucking her fingers.

The older sister looked but saw nothing. She did not see the unripe bananas like stubby fingers hanging down, which had been there when she went to get the water; she did not see the peels, which she would find later in the garbage.

There was a monkey, the little sister said. A tiny, tiny monkey. It had fingers like person fingers. It sat on the roof and peeled the bananas and ate them all up.

The older girl looked at the little sister. She stared back with round eyes. There was a long silence, and something in the older sister turned away, even as she nodded.

All right, then. There was a monkey.

Now, over the wind, all the way across the pond, from the beach on the other side of the island, there came a noise the older sister caught, then lost, then caught again. It was a song their mother had often sung along to on the radio in the car. A song—that meant a radio. The older girl took her sister's face in her hands. We got to get ready fast, she said. Then we got to run.

———

They scrubbed themselves in the waves and, wet, put on their mother's dresses, the only clean things there were. Shifts in tropical patterns that came down below the older girl's knees, to the younger one's ankles; on their mother those dresses were so short you could sometimes see her underwear when she was sitting down. They poured her perfume all over their wrists and heads.

Then they ran. They stopped when they were still among the trees, breathing heavily.

There was a boat anchored not far out, and a rubber dinghy pulled up on the wet part of the sand and a fishing pole buried next to it. A woman lay on a blanket. She was white, though her shoulders and thighs were going pink. She was plump. She was mouthing along to a different song on the radio, her feet waggling back and forth in time.

There was a man beside the dinghy with his swimming trunks down to his knees. He was peeing, the girls saw. He didn't even wash his hands in the waves, but went over to the woman and stooped and put them in a cooler for a minute, then popped them under the woman's bikini bottom while she screamed and swatted at him.

He laughed and took a beer can from the cooler and opened it and drank deeply, and picked up a sandwich in waxed paper. The older sister's mouth watered. She was glad when he crumpled the paper up and didn't litter but put it neatly back into the cooler.

The older girl looked at her sister. She was wild. You could see all her bones. The older sister took the brown leaves out of the little one's hair, brushed the dirt off her dress, took out their mother's lipstick, which she'd put into her pocket as they ran out the door. She put lipstick on her sister's lips, then made tiny circles on her cheeks. Now me, she ordered, and her little sister's face pursed in concentration and the lipstick tickled on her own cheeks and lips.

She put the lipstick back into her pocket. She would keep the gold cartridge of it long after the makeup inside was gone and only a sweet waxy smell of her mother remained.

Ready? she said. Her sister nodded and took her hand. Together they stepped out of the shadows and onto the blazing beach.

The woman on the blanket looked up at them, then shaded her eyes with a hand to see better. Later the woman would visit the girls once, then disappear after she left the older sister a gift, a vision of how the sisters had looked just then: ghost girls in clown makeup and floral sacks, creeping out of the dark forest. The woman's mouth opened and a cry of alarm stuck in her throat. She raised her arms in amazement. The girls took the gesture for a welcome. Though they were very tired and felt tiny under the angry sun, they ran.

THE MIDNIGHT ZONE

———

I t was an old hunting camp shipwrecked in twenty miles
of scrub. Our friend had seen a Florida panther sliding
through the trees there a few days earlier. But things
had been fraying in our hands, and the camp was free and
silent, so I walked through the resistance of my cautious
husband and my small boys, who had wanted hermit
crabs and kites and wakeboards and sand for spring break.
Instead, they got ancient sinkholes filled with ferns, po-
tential death by cat.

One thing I liked was how the screens at night pulsed
with the tender bellies of lizards.

Even in the sleeping bag with my smaller son, the
golden one, the March chill seemed to blow through my
bones. I loved eating, but I'd lost so much weight by then
that I carried myself delicately, as if I'd gone translucent.

There was sparse electricity from a gas-powered generator and no Internet, and you had to climb out through

the window in the loft and stand on the roof to get a cell signal. On the third day, the boys were asleep and I'd dimmed the lanterns when my husband went up and out, and I heard him stepping on the metal roof, a giant brother to the raccoons that woke us thumping around up there at night like burglars.

Then my husband stopped moving, and stood still for so long I forgot where he was. When he came down the ladder from the loft, his face had blanched.

Who died? I said lightly, because if anyone was going to die it was going to be us, our skulls popping in the jaws of an endangered cat. It turned out to be a bad joke, because someone actually had died, that morning, in one of my husband's apartment buildings. A fifth-floor occupant had killed herself, maybe on purpose, with aspirin and vodka and a bathtub. Floors four, three, and two were away somewhere with beaches and alcoholic smoothies, and the first floor had discovered the problem only when the water of death had seeped into the carpet.

My husband had to leave. He'd just fired one handyman, and the other was on his own Caribbean adventure, eating buffet foods to the sound of cruise-ship calypso. Let's pack, my husband said, but my rebelliousness at the time was like a sticky fog rolling through my body and never burning off, there was no sun inside, and so I said that the boys and I would stay. He looked at me as if I were crazy and asked how we'd manage with no car. I asked if he thought he'd married an incompetent woman, which cut to the bone, because the source of our problems was that, in fact, he had. For years at a time I was good only at the things that interested me, and since all that interested me was my books and my children, the rest of life had sort of inched away. And while it's true that my children were endlessly fascinating, two petri dishes growing human cultures, being a mother never had been, and all that seemed assigned by default of gender I would not do because it felt insulting. I would not buy clothes, I would not make dinner, I would not keep schedules, I would not make playdates, never ever. Motherhood meant, for me, that I would take the boys on monthlong adventures to Europe, teach them to blast off rockets, to swim for glory. I taught them how to read, but they could make their own lunches. I would hug them as long as they wanted to be hugged, but that was just being human. My husband had to be the one to make up for the depths of my lack. It is exhausting, living in debt that increases every day but that you have no intention of repaying.

Two days, he promised. Two days and he'd be back by noon on the third. He bent to kiss me, but I gave him my cheek and rolled over when the headlights blazed then dwindled on the wall. In the banishing of the engine, the night grew bold. The wind was making a low, inhuman muttering in the pines, and, inspired, the animals let loose in call-and-response. Everything kept me alert until shortly before dawn, when I slept for a few minutes until the puppy whined and woke me. My older son was crying because he'd thrown off his sleeping bag in the night and was cold but too sleepy to fix the situation.

I made scrambled eggs with a vengeful amount of butter and cheddar, also cocoa with an inch of marshmallow, thinking I would stupefy my children with calories, but the calories only made them stronger.

Our friend had treated the perimeter of the clearing with panther deterrent, some kind of synthetic superpredator urine, and we felt safe-ish near the cabin. We ran footraces until the dog went wild and leapt up and bit my children's arms with her puppy teeth, and the boys screamed with pain and frustration and showed me the pink stripes on their skin. I scolded the puppy harshly and she crept off to the porch to watch us with her chin on her paws. The boys and I played soccer. We rocked in the hammock. We watched the circling red-winged hawks. I made my older son read *Alice's Adventures in Wonderland* to the little one, which was a disaster, a book so punny and Victorian for modern cartoonish children. We had lunch, then the older boy tried to make fire by rubbing sticks together, his little brother attending solemnly, and they spent the rest of the day constructing a hut out of branches. Then dinner, singing songs, a bath in the galvanized-steel horse trough someone had converted to a cold-water tub, picking ticks and chiggers off with tweezers, and that was it for the first day.

There had been a weight on us as we played outside, not as if something were actually watching, but merely the possibility that something could be watching when we were so far from humanity in all that Florida waste.

The second day should have been like the first. I doubled down on calories, adding pancakes to breakfast, and succeeded in making the boys lie in pensive digestion out in the hammock for a little while before they ricocheted off the trees.

But in the afternoon the one lightbulb sizzled out. The cabin was all dark wood, and I couldn't see the patterns on the dishes I was washing. I found a new bulb in a closet and dragged over a stool from the bar area and made the older boy hold the spinning seat as I climbed aboard. The old bulb was hot, and I was passing it from hand to hand, holding the new bulb under my arm, when the puppy leapt up at my older son's face. He let go of the stool to whack at her, and I did a quarter spin, then fell and hit the floor with my head, and then I surely blacked out.

After a while, I opened my eyes. Two children were looking down at me. They were pale and familiar. One fair, one dark; one small, one big.

Mommy? the little boy said, through water.

I turned my head and threw up on the floor. The bigger boy dragged a puppy, who was snuffling my face, out the door.

I knew very little except that I was in pain and that I

shouldn't move. The older boy bent over me, then lifted an intact lightbulb from my armpit triumphantly; I a chicken, the bulb an egg.

The smaller boy had a wet paper towel in his hand and he was patting my cheeks. The pulpy smell made me ill again. I closed my eyes and felt the dabbing on my forehead, on my neck, around my mouth. The small child's voice was high. He was singing a song.

I started to cry with my eyes closed and the tears went hot across my temples and into my ears.

Mommy! the older boy, the solemn dark one, screamed, and when I opened my eyes, both of the children were crying, and that was how I knew them to be mine.

Just let me rest here a minute, I said. They took my hands. I could feel the hot hands of my children, which was good. I moved my toes, then my feet. I turned my head back and forth. My neck worked, though fireworks went off in the corners of my eyes.

I can walk to town, the older boy was saying to his brother through wadding, but the nearest town was twenty miles away. Safety was twenty miles away and there was a panther between us and there, but also possibly terrible men, sinkholes, alligators, the end of the world. There was no landline, no umbilicus, and small boys using cell phones would easily fall off such a slick, pitched metal roof.

But what if she's all a sudden dead and I'm all a sudden alone? the little boy was saying.

Okay, I'm sitting up now, I said.

The puppy was howling at the door.

I lifted my body onto my elbows. Gingerly, I sat. The cabin dipped and spun, and I vomited again.

The big boy ran out and came back with a broom to clean up. No! I said. I am always too hard on him, this beautiful child who is so brilliant, who has no logic at all.

Sweetness, I said, and I couldn't stop crying, because I'd called him Sweetness instead of his name, which I couldn't remember just then. I took five or six deep breaths. Thank you, I said in a calmer voice. Just throw a whole bunch of paper towels on it and drag the rug over it to keep the dog off. The little one did so, methodically, which was not his style; he has always been adept at cheerfully watching other people work for him.

The bigger boy tried to get me to drink water, because this is what we do in our family in lieu of applying Band-Aids, which I refuse to buy because they are just flesh-colored landfill.

Then the little boy screamed, because he'd moved around me and seen the bloody back of my head, and then he dabbed at the cut with the paper towel he had previously dabbed at my pukey mouth. The paper disintegrated in his hands. He crawled into my lap and put his face on my stomach. The bigger boy held something cold on my wound, which I discovered later to be a beer can from the fridge.

They were quiet like this for a very long time. The

boys' names came back to me, at first dancing coyly out of reach, then, when I seized them in my hands, mine.

I'd been a soccer player in high school, a speedy and aggressive midfielder, and head trauma was an old friend. I remembered this constant lability from one concussive visit to the emergency room. The confusion and the sense of doom were also familiar. I had a flash of my mother sitting beside my bed for an entire night, shaking me awake whenever I tried to fall asleep, and I wanted my mother, not in her diminished current state, brittle retiree, but as she had been when I was young, a small person but gigantic, a person who had blocked out the sun.

I sent the little boy off to get a roll of dusty duct tape, the bigger boy to get gauze from my toiletry kit, and when they wandered back, I duct-taped the gauze to my head, already mourning my long hair, which had been my most expensive pet.

I inched myself across the room to the bed and climbed up, despite the sparklers behind my eyeballs. The boys let the forlorn puppy in, and when they opened the door they also let the night in, because my fall had taken hours from our lives.

It was only then, when the night entered, that I understood the depth of time we had yet to face. I had the boys bring me the lanterns, then a can opener and the tuna and the beans, which I opened slowly, because it is not easy, supine, and we made a game out of eating, though the thought of eating anything gave me chills. The older boy brought over mason jars of milk. I let my children finish the entire half gallon of ice cream, which was my husband's, his one daily reward for being kind and good, but by this point the man deserved our disloyalty, because he was not there.

It had started raining, at first a gentle thrumming on the metal roof.

I tried to tell my children a cautionary tale about a little girl who fell into a well and had to wait a week until firefighters could figure out a way to rescue her, something that maybe actually took place back in the dimness of my childhood, but the story was either too abstract for them or I wasn't making much sense, and they didn't seem to grasp my need for them to stay in the cabin, to not go anywhere, if the very worst happened, the unthinkable that I was skirting, like a pit that opened just in front of each sentence I was about to utter. They kept asking me if the girl got lots of toys when she made it out of the well. This was so against my point that I said, out of spite, Unfortunately, no, she did not.

I made the boys keep me awake with stories. The younger one was into a British television show about marine life, which the older one maintained was babyish until I pretended not to believe what they were telling me. Then they both told me about cookie-cutter sharks, which bore perfect round holes in whales, as if their mouths were cookie cutters. They told me about a fish called the humuhumunukunukuāpua'a, a beautiful name that I couldn't say correctly, even though they sang it to me over and over, laughing, to the tune of "Twinkle, Twinkle, Little Star." They told me about the walking catfish, which can stay out of water for three days, meandering about in the mud. They told me about the sunlight, the twilight, and the midnight zones, the three densities of water, where there is transparent light, then a murky darkish light, then no light at all. They told me about the World Pool, in which one current goes one way, another goes another way, and where they meet they make a tornado of air, which stretches, said my little one, from the midnight zone, where the fish are blind, all the way up up up to the birds.

I had begun shaking very hard, which my children, sudden gentlemen, didn't mention. They piled all the sleeping bags and blankets on me, then climbed under and fell asleep without bathing or toothbrushing or getting out of their dirty clothes, which, anyway, they sweated through within an hour.

The dog did not get dinner but she didn't whine about it, and though she wasn't allowed to, she came up on the bed and slept with her head on my older son's stomach, because he was her favorite, being the biggest puppy of all.

Now I had only myself to sit vigil with me, though it was still early, nine or ten at night.

I had a European novel on the nightstand that filled me with bleach and fret, so I tried to read *Alice's Adventures in Wonderland*, but it was incomprehensible with my scrambled brains. Then I looked at a hunting magazine, which made me remember the Florida panther. I hadn't truly forgotten it, but I could manage only a few terrors at a time, and others, when my children had been awake, were more urgent. We had seen some scat in the woods on a walk three days earlier, enormous scat, either a bear's or the panther's, but certainly a giant carnivore's. The danger had been abstract until we saw this bodily proof of existence, and my husband and I led the children home, singing a round, all four of us holding hands, and we let the dog off the leash to circle us joyously, because, as small as she was, it was bred in her bones that in the face of peril she would sacrifice herself first.

The rain increased until it was loud and still my sweaty children slept. I thought of the waves of sleep rushing through their brains, washing out the tiny unimportant flotsam of today so that tomorrow's heavier truths could wash in. There was a nice solidity to the rain's pounding on the roof, as if the noise were a barrier that nothing could enter, a stay against the looming night.

I tried to bring back the poems of my youth, and could not remember more than a few floating lines, which I put together into a strange, sad poem, Blake and Dickinson and Frost and Milton and Sexton, a tag-sale poem in clammy meter that nonetheless came alive and held my hand for a little while.

Then the rain diminished until all that was left were

scattered clicks from the drops drifting off the pines. The batteries of one lantern went out and the light from the remaining lantern was sparse and thwarted. I could hardly see my hand or the shadow it made on the wall when I held it up. This lantern was my sister; at any moment it, too, could go dark. I feasted my eyes on the cabin, which in the oncoming black had turned into a place made of gold, but the shadows seemed too thick now, fizzy at the edges, and they moved when I shifted my eyes away from them. It felt safer to look at the cheeks of my sleeping children, creamy as cheeses.

It was elegiac, that last hour or so of light, and I tried to push my love for my sons into them where their bodies were touching my own skin.

The wind rose again and it had personality; it was in a sharpish, meanish mood. It rubbed itself against the little cabin and played at the corners and broke sticks off the trees and tossed them at the roof so they jigged down like creatures with strange and scrabbling claws. The wind rustled its endless body against the door.

Everything depended on my staying still, but my skin was stuffed with itches. Something terrible in me, the darkest thing, wanted to slam my own head back against the headboard. I imagined it over and over, the sharp backward crack, and the wash and spill of peace.

I counted slow breaths and was not calm by two hundred; I counted to a thousand.

The lantern flicked itself out and the dark poured in.

The moon rose in the skylight and backed itself across the black.

When it was gone and I was alone again, I felt the disassociation, a physical shifting, as if the best of me were detaching from my body and sitting down a few feet distant. It was a great relief.

For a few moments, there was a sense of mutual watching, a wait for something definitive, though nothing definitive came, and then the bodiless me stood and circled the cabin. The dog shifted and gave a soft whine through her nose, although she remained asleep. The floors were cool underfoot. My head brushed the beams, though they were ten feet up. Where my body and those of my two sons lay together was a black and pulsing mass, a hole of light.

I passed outside. The path was pale dirt and filled with sandspurs and was cold and wet after the rain. The great drops from the tree branches left a pine taste in me. The forest was not dark, because darkness has nothing to do with the forest—the forest is made of life, of light—but the trees moved with wind and subtle creatures. I wasn't in any single place. I was with the raccoons of the rooftop that were now down fiddling with the bicycle lock on the garbage can at the end of the road, with the red-winged hawk chicks breathing alone in the nest, with the armadillo forcing its armored body through the brush. I hadn't realized that I'd lost my sense of smell until it returned hungrily now; I could smell the worms tracing their paths under the pine needles and the mold breathing out new spores, shaken alive by the rain.

I was vigilant, moving softly in the underbrush, and the palmettos' nails scraped down my body.

The cabin was not visible, but it was present, a sore at my side, a feeling of density and airlessness. I couldn't go away from it, I couldn't return, I could only circle the cabin and circle it. With each circle, a terrible, stinging anguish built in me and I had to move faster and faster, each pass bringing up ever more wildness. What had been built to seem so solid was fragile in the face of time because time is impassive, more animal than human. Time would not care if you fell out of it. It would continue on without you. It cannot see you; it has always been blind to the human and the things we do to stave it off, the taxonomies, the cleaning, the arranging, the ordering. Even this cabin with its perfectly considered angles, its veins of pipes and wires, was barely more stable than the rake marks we made in the dust that morning, which time had already scrubbed away.

The self in the woods ran and ran, but the running couldn't hold off the slow shift. A low mist rose from the ground and gradually came clearer. The first birds sent their questions into the chilly air. The sky developed its blue. The sun emerged.

The drawing back was gradual. My older son opened his brown eyes and saw me sitting above him.

You look terrible, he said, patting my face, and my hearing was only half underwater now.

My head ached, so I held my mouth shut and smiled with my eyes and he padded off to the kitchen and came back with peanut-butter-and-jelly sandwiches, with a set of Uno cards, with cold coffee from yesterday's pot for the low and constant thunder of my headache, with the dog whom he'd let out and then fed all by himself.

I watched him. He gleamed. My little son woke but didn't get up, as if his face were attached to my shoulder by the skin. He was rubbing one unbloodied lock of my hair on his lips, the way he did after he nursed when he was a baby.

My boys were not unhappy. I was usually a preoccupied mother, short with them, busy, working, until I burst into fun, then went back to my hole of work; now I could only sit with them, talk to them. I could not even read. They were gentle with me, reminded me of a golden retriever I'd grown up with, a dog with a mouth so soft she would go down to the lake and steal ducklings and hold them intact on her tongue for hours until we noticed her sitting unusually erect in the corner, looking sly. My boys were like their father; they would one day be men who would take care of the people they loved.

I closed my eyes as the boys played game after game after game of Uno.

Noon arrived, noon left, and my husband did not come.

At one point, something passed across the woods outside like a shudder, and everything went quiet, and the boys and the dog all looked at me and their faces were like pale birds taking flight, but my hearing had mercifully shut off whatever had occasioned such swift terror over all creatures of the earth, save me.

When we heard the car from afar at four in the afternoon, the boys jumped up. They burst out of the cabin, leaving the door wide open to the blazing light that hurt my eyes. I heard their father's voice, and then his footsteps, and he was running, and behind him the boys were running, the dog was running. Here were my husband's feet on the dirt drive. Here were his feet heavy on the porch.

For a half breath, I would have vanished myself. I was everything we had fretted about, this passive Queen of Chaos with her bloody duct-tape crown. My husband filled the door. He is a man born to fill doors. I shut my eyes. When I opened them, he was enormous above me. In his face was a thing that made me go quiet inside, made a long, slow sizzle creep up my arms from the fingertips, because the thing I read in his face was the worst, it was fear, and it was vast, it was elemental, like the wind itself, like the cold sun I would soon feel on the silk of my pelt.

EYEWALL

=====

t began with the chickens. They were Rhode Island Reds and I'd raised them from chicks. Though I called until my voice gave out, they'd huddled in the darkness under the house, a dim mass faintly pulsing. Fine, you ungrateful turds! I'd said before abandoning them to the storm. I stood in the kitchen at the one window I'd left unboarded and watched the hurricane's bruise spreading in the west. I felt the chickens' fear rising through the floorboards to pass through me like prayers.

We waited. The weatherman on the television repeated the swirl of the hurricane with his body like a valiant but inept mime. All the other creatures of the earth flattened themselves, dug in. I stood in my window watching, a captain at the wheel, as the first gust filled the oaks on the far side of the lake and raced across the water. It shivered my lawn, my garden, sent the unplucked zucchini swinging like church bells. And then the wind smacked the house. Bring it on! I shouted. Or, just maybe, this is another thing in my absurd life that I whispered.

At first, though, little happened. The lake goose-bumped; I might have been looking at the sensitive flesh of an enormous lizard. The swing in the oak made larger arcs over the water. The palmettos nodded, accepting the dance.

The wine I had been drinking was very good. I opened another bottle. It had been left in a special cooler in the butler's pantry that had been designed to replicate precisely the earthy damp of the *caves* under Bourgogne. One bottle cost a year of retirement, or an hour squinting down the barrel of a hurricane.

My neighbor's jeep kicked up hillocks of pale dust on the road. He saw me standing in the window and skidded to a halt. He rolled down his own window and shouted, and his face squared into his neck, which was the warm hue of a brick. But the wind now was so loud that his voice was lost, and I felt a surge of affection for him as he leaned out the window, gesticulating. We'd had a moment a few years back at a Conservation Trust benefit just after my husband left, our fortyish bodies both stuffed into finery. There was the taste of whiskey and the weirdness of his moustache against my teeth. Now I toasted him with my glass, and he shouted so hard he turned purple, and his hunting dog stuck her head out the back window and began to howl. I raised two fingers and calmly gave him a pope's blessing. He bulged, affronted, and rolled up his window. He made a gesture as if wadding up a hunk of paper and tossing it behind his shoulder, and then he pulled away to join the last stragglers pushing north as fast as their engines could strain. The great rag of the storm would wipe them off the road. I'd hear of the way my neighbor's jeep, going a hundred miles per hour, lovingly kissed the concrete riser of an overpass. His dog would land clear over the six lanes in the southbound culvert and dig herself down. When the night passed and the day dawned calm, she'd pull herself to the road and find herself the sole miraculous survivor of a mile-long flesh-and-metal sandwich.

began to sing to myself, songs from childhood, songs with lyrics I didn't understand then and still don't, folk songs and commercial jingles and the Hungarian lullaby my father sang during my many sleepless nights when I was small. I was a high-strung, beetle-browed girl, and the songs only made me want to stay awake longer, to outlast him until he fell asleep crookedly against my headboard and I could watch the way his dreams moved beneath his handsome face. Enervated and watchful in school the next day, I'd be unable to follow the teacher's voice, the ropes of her sentences as she led us through history or English or math, and I would fill my notebooks with drawings—a hundred different houses, floors and windows and doors. All day I'd furiously scribble. If I only drew the right place to hold me, I could escape from the killing hours of school and draw myself all the way safely home.

The house sucked in a shuddery breath, and the plywood groaned as the windows drew inward. Darkness fell over the world outside. Rain unleashed itself. It was neither freight train nor jet engine nor cataract crashing around me but, rather, everything. The roof roared with water, the window blurred. When the storm cleared, I saw a branch the size of a locomotive cracking off the heritage oak by the lake and falling languorously down, the wet moss floating outstretched like useless dark wings.

I felt, rather than saw, the power go out. Time erased itself from the appliances and the lights winked shut. The house went sinister behind me, oppressive with its dark humidity. When I turned, I saw my husband in the far doorway.

You're drinking my wine, he said. I could hear him perfectly, despite the storm. He was a stumpy man, thirty years older than me. I could smell the mint sprigs he chewed and the skin ointment for his psoriasis.

I didn't think you'd mind, I said. You don't need it anymore.

He put both hands over his chest and smiled. A week after he left me, his heart broke itself apart. He was in bed with his mistress. She was so preposterously young that I assumed they conversed in baby talk. He hadn't wanted children until he ended up fucking one. I was glad that she was the one who'd had to be stuck under his moist and cooling body, the one to shout his name and have it go unanswered.

He came closer and stood next to me in the window. I went very still, as I always did near him. We watched the world on its bender outside. My beautiful tomatoes had flattened and the metal cages minced away across the lawn, as if ghosts were wearing them as hoop skirts.

You're still here, of course, he said. Even though they told you to get out days ago.

This house is old, I said. It has lived through other storms.

You never listen to anyone, he said.

Have some wine, I said. Stand with me. Watch the show. But for God's sake, shut it.

He looked at me deeply. He had huge brown eyes that were young no matter how alligatored his skin got. His eyes were what had made me fall for him. He was a very good poet. The night I met him, I sat spellbound at a reading my friend had dragged me to, his words softening the ground of me, so that when he looked up, those brown eyes could tunnel all the way through.

He drank a swig of wine and moaned in appreciation. At its peak, he said. Perfection. Drink it now.

I plan to, I said.

He began to go vague on me. I knew his poems were no good when they began to go vague. How's my reputation? he said, the fingers of his hands melding into mittens. I was his literary executor; he hadn't had time to change that one last thing.

I'm letting it languish, I said.

Ah, he said. *La belle dame sans merci.*

I don't speak Italian, I said.

French, he said.

Oh, dear, I said. My ignorance must have been so maddening.

Honey, he said, you don't know the half of it.

Well, I said. I *do* know my half.

I didn't say, I had never said: Lord, how I longed for a version of you I could hold, entire, in my arms.

He winked at me, and the mint smell intensified, and there was a pressure on my mouth, then a lessening. And then it was only the storm and the house and me.

The darkness redoubled, the sound intensified. There were pulsing navy veins within the clouds; I remembered a hunting trip with my husband once, the buck's organs gutted onto the ground. The camphor and magnolia and crape myrtles pressed their crowns to the earth, backbending, acrobats. My teak picnic table galumphed itself toward the road, chasing after the chairs already fled that way.

My best laying hen was scraped from under the house and slid in a horrifying diagonal across the window. For a moment, we were eye to lizardy eye. I took a breath. The glass fogged, and when it cleared, my hen had blown away. Then the top layer of the lake seemed to rise in one great sheet and crush itself against the house. When the wind swept the water into the road, my garden became a pit in which a gar twisted and a baby alligator dug furiously into the mud. From behind the flattened blueberries, a nightmare creature of mud stood and leaned against the wind. It showed itself to be a man only moments before the wind picked him up and slammed him into the door. I didn't think before I ran and heaved it open so the man could tumble in. I was blown off my feet and had to clutch the doorknob to keep from flying. The wind seized a flowerpot and smashed it through the microwave. The man crawled and helped me push the door until at last it closed and the storm was banished, howling to find itself outside again.

The man was mudstruck, naked, laughing. A gold curl emerged from the filth of his head, and I wiped his face with the hem of my dress until I saw that he was my college boyfriend. I sat down on the floor beside him, scrabbling the dirt from him with my fingernails until I could make him out in his entirety.

Oh! he shouted when he could speak. He'd always been a cheery boy, talkative and loving. He clutched my face between his hands and said, You're old! You're old! You should wear the bottoms of your trousers rolled.

I don't wear trousers, I said, and snatched my head away. There was still water in the pipes, and I washed him until he was clean. He fashioned a loincloth out of a kitchen towel. He kept his head turned from me, staring at me from the corners of his eyes until I took his chin in my fingers and turned it. There it was, the wet rose blossoming above his ear. He took a long swallow of wine, and I watched a red ligament move over the bone.

So you really did it, I said.

A friend of a friend of a friend had told me something: Calgary, the worst motel he could find, the family's antique dueling pistol. But I didn't trust either the friend or the friend of the friend, certainly not the friend to the third power, and this act seemed so out of character for such a vivid soul that I decided it couldn't possibly have been true.

It's so strange, I said. You were always the happiest person I knew. You were so happy I had to break up with you.

He cocked his head and pulled me into his lap. Happy, eh? he said.

I rested against his thin young chest. I thought of how I had been so tired after two years of him, how I couldn't bear the three a.m. phone calls when he *had* to read me a passage from Benjamin, the Saturdays when I had to search for him in bars or find him in strangers' living rooms, how, if I had to make one more goddamn egg sandwich to fill his mouth and quiet him and make him fall asleep at dawn, I would shatter into fragments myself. Our last month was in Spain. I had sold one of my ovaries to get us there, and lost him in Barcelona. For an hour, I wept at the center of a knot of concerned Spaniards until he came loping down the street toward me, some stranger's stolen Afghan hound tugging at the leash in his hand. A light had been kindled in his eye; it blazed before him, a herald announcing his peculiar self. I looked up at him in the dim of the stormstruck house, the hole in the side of his head.

He smiled, expectant, brushing my knuckles with his lips. I said, Oh.

Bygones, he said. He downed half of the bottle of wine as if it were a plastic cup of beer. A swarm of palmetto bugs burst up through the air-conditioning vent and paraded by in single file, giving the impression of politeness. I could feel the thinness of the towel between his skin and my legs, the way this beautiful boy had always stirred me.

My God, I loved you, I said. I had played it close to my chest then; I had thought not telling him was the source of my power over him.

Also bygones, he said. Now tell me what you're doing here.

The rowboat skipped over the lake, waggling its oars

like swimmers' arms. It launched itself into the trunks of the oaks and pinned itself there. I saw the glass of the window beating, darkness so deep in it that I could see myself, gray at the temples, lined from nostril to lip. The house felt cavernous around me. I had thought it would be full by now: of husband, of small voices, at the very least of chickens.

Do you remember our children? I asked.

He beamed. Clothilde, he said. Rupert. Haricot and Abricot, the twins. Dodie. Australopithecus. And Dirk. All prodigies, with your brains and my looks.

You forgot Cleanth, I said.

My favorite! he said. How could I have forgotten? Maker of crossword puzzles, National Spelling Bee champion. Good old Cleanth.

He lifted the back of my hand to his lips and kissed it. It's too bad, he murmured.

Before I could ask what was too bad, the window imploded, showering us with glass. The wind reached in and sucked him out. I clutched at the countertops and saw my beautiful boy swan-dive into the three-foot-deep pond that had been my yard. He turned on his back and did a few strokes. Then he imitated one of my dead chickens floating about in the water, her two wings cocked skyward in imprecation. Like synchronized swimmers, they swirled about each other, arms to the sky, and then, in a gulp, both sank.

tucked two bottles and a corkscrew into my sleeves and pulled myself to the doorway against the tug of the wind. I could barely walk when I was through. The house heaved around me and the wind followed, over-turning clocks and chairs, paging through the sheet mu-sic on the piano before snatching it up and carrying it away. It riffled through my books one by one as if search-ing for marginalia, then toppled the bookshelves. The water pushed upward from under the house, through the floorcracks, through the vents, turning my rugs into marshes. Rats scampered up the stairs to my bedroom. I trudged over the mess and crawled up, step by step, on my hands and knees. A terrapin passed me, then a raccoon with a baby clutched to its back, gazing at me with wide robber's eyes. Peekaboo, I said, and it hid its face in its mother's ruff. In the light of a battery-powered alarm clock, I saw rats, a snake, a possum, a heap of bugs scat-tered across the room, as if gathered for a slumber party, all those gleaming eyes in the dark. The bathroom was the sole windowless place at the heart of the house, and when I was inside, I locked them all out.

sat in the bathtub, loving its cool embrace of my body. I have always felt a sisterhood with bathtubs; without someone else within us, we are smooth white cups of nothing. It was thick black in the bathroom, sealed tight. The house twisted and shook; above, the roof peeled itself slowly apart. The wind played the chimney until the whole place wheezed like a bagpipe. I savored each sip of wine and wondered what the end would be: the roof gone and the storm galloping in; the house tilting on its risers and rolling me out; a water moccasin crawling up the pipes and finding a warm place to nest between my legs.

Above the scream of the storm, there came the hiss and sputter of a wet match. Then a weak flame licked brightly near the toilet and went out. There rose in its place the sweet smell of pipe smoke.

Jesus Christ, I said.

No. Your father, he said in his soft accent. He had a smile in his voice when he said, Watch your language, my love.

I felt him near, sitting at the edge of the bathtub as if it were the side of a bed. I felt his hand brushing the wet hair out of my mouth. I lifted my own hand and caught his, feeling the sop of his flesh against the fragile bone. I was glad it was dark. He'd been eaten from the inside by cancer. My mother, after too many gin and tonics, always turned cruel. She had once described my father's end to me. The last few days, she'd said, he was a sack of swollen flesh.

I hadn't been there. I didn't even know he was sick. I'd been sent to Girl Scout camp. While he slowly died, I learned how to tie knots. While he hallucinated about his village, the cherry trees, the bull in the field that bellowed at night for sex, I kissed a girl named Julia Pfeffernuss. I believed for years afterward that tongues should taste like the clovers we'd sucked for the honey at their roots. When my father was forgetting his English and shouting for his mother in Hungarian, I stole a sailboat and went alone to the quiet heart of the reservoir. Before the dam had been built, there had been a village there. I took down the sails and dropped the anchor and dove. I opened my eyes to find myself outside a young girl's room, her brushes and combs still laid out on her vanity, me in the algaed mirror, framed by the window. I saw a catfish lying on a platter in the dining room as if serving himself up; he looked at me and shook his head and sagely swam away. I saw sheets forgotten on the line, waving upward toward the sun. I came out of the lake and climbed into the boat and tacked for camp, and didn't tell a soul what I had seen, never, not once, not even my husband, who would have made it his own.

I might have told my friends at camp, I think. I don't think I'd meant to keep the miracle to myself. But the camp's director had been waiting for me on the dock, a hungry pity pressing her lips thin, the red hood of her sweatshirt waggled in the air behind her. It stirred still, in my memory, a big and ugly tongue.

When we first saw this house on its sixty acres, I didn't fall for the heart-pine floors or the attic fan that kept the house cool all summer without air-conditioning or the magnolias blooming their goblets of white light. I fell for the long swing in the heritage oak over the lake, which had thrilled some child, which was waiting for another. My husband looked at the study, mahogany-paneled, and said under his breath, Yes. I stood in the kitchen and looked at the swing, at the way the sun hit the wood so gently, the promise it held, and thought, Yes. Every day for ten years, watching the swing move expectantly in the light wind of morning, thinking, Yes, the word quietly piercing the diaphragm, that same Yes until the day my husband left, and even after he left, and then even after he died; even then, still hoping.

For a very long time, we sat there like that: my dad's hand in mine, in the roaring black. I waited for him to speak, but he had always been a man who knew how to groom the silence between people. He smoked, I drank, and the world tired itself out with its tantrum.

I lost awareness of my body. There was only the smoothness of the porcelain beneath me, the warmth of my father's hand. Time passed, endless, a breath.

Slowly, the wind softened. Sobbed. Stopped. The house trembled and moaned itself back to pitch. A trickle of dawn painted a gray strip under the door. My body returned to itself. I could hear only my heartbeat and rain off the roof when I said, Remember when you used to call your family in Hungary?

You were always so furious, he said. You would scream at me when I tried to talk. Your mother had to take you out to get ice cream every time I wanted to call.

I couldn't eat it. I just watched it melt, I said.

I know, he said.

I still can't eat it, I said. I hated that you opened your mouth and suddenly became another person.

We waited. The air felt poached, both sticky and wet. I said, I never thought I could be so alone.

We're all alone, he said.

You had me, I said.

True, he said. He squeezed the back of my neck, kneaded the knots out.

I listened to the shifting of the world outside. This is either the eye or we've made it through, I said.

Well, he said. There will always be another storm, you know.

I stood, woozy, the bottles clanking off my body back into the bathtub. I know, I said.

You'll be A-OK, he said.

That's no wisdom coming from you, I said. Everything's all right for the dead.

When I opened the door to the bedroom, the room was blazing with light. The plywood over the windows had caught the wind like sails and carried the frames from the house. There were rectangular holes in the wall. The creatures had left the room. The storm had stripped the sheets like a good guest, and they had all blown away, save one, which hung pale and perfect over the mirror, saving myself from the sight of me.

The damage was done: three-hundred-year-old trees smashed, towns flattened as if a fist had come from the sun and twisted. My life was scattered into three counties. Someone found a novel with my bookplate in it sunning itself on top of a car in Georgia. Everywhere I looked, the dead. A neighbor child, come through the storm, had wandered outside while the rest of the family was salvaging what remained, and had fallen into the pool and drowned. The high school basketball team, ignoring all warnings, crossed a bridge and was swallowed up by the Gulf. Old friends were carried away on the floods; others, seeing the little that remained, let their hearts break. The storm had stolen the rest of the wine and the butler's pantry, too. My chickens had drowned, blown apart, their feathers freckling the ground. For weeks, the stench of their rot would fill my dreams. Over the next month, mold would eat its way up the plaster and leave gorgeous abstract murals of sage and burnt sienna behind. But the frame had held, the doors had held. The house, in the end, had held.

On my way downstairs, I passed a congregation of exhausted armadillos on the landing. Birds had filled the

Florida room, cardinals and whip-poor-wills and owls. Gently, the insects fled from my step. I sloshed over the rugs that bled their vegetable dyes onto the floorboards. My brain was too small for my skull and banged from side to side as I walked. Moving in the humidity was like forcing my way through wet silk. Still, I opened the door to look at the devastation outside.

And there I stopped, breathless. I laughed. Isn't this the fucking kicker, I said aloud. Or maybe I didn't.

Houses contain us; who can say what we contain? Out where the steps had been, balanced beside the drop-off: one egg, whole and mute, holding all the light of dawn in its skin.

FOR THE GOD OF LOVE,
FOR THE LOVE OF GOD

═══════

S tone house down a gully of grapevines. Under the roof, a great pale room.

Night had been drawn out by the way the house eclipsed the dawn. Morning came when the sun flared against the hill and suddenly shone in. What had begun as a joke in the dark came clear to the man in the fields who was riding a strange sort of tractor that straddled the vines. He idled, parallel the window, to watch. Amanda thought this was a very French thing to do. The heat in her face was not because of the nudity; rather, the plagiarism. Her idea had come from the tractor's first squatting pass in the window. She slapped her husband's stomach below and said, Finish.

A minute later she strode off the bed and went to the window and, leaning for the curtains on each side, pressed her chest against the glass, to tease. The man on the tractor wasn't a man but a young boy. He was laughing.

In the curtained dark again, they heard the tractor moving off, then the flurries of roosters down in the village.

Nice surprise, Grant said, sliding his hand down her thigh. Hope we didn't wake them up. He stretched, lazy. Amanda imagined their hosts in the room below: Manfred staring blankly at the wall. Drooling. Genevieve with her passive-aggressive buzzing beneath the duvet.

Who cares, Amanda said.

Well, Grant said. There's Leo, too.

I forgot, she said.

Poor kid, Grant said. Everyone always forgets about Leo.

Amanda went down the stairs in her running clothes. She passed Leo's room, then doubled back.

Leo stood on the high window ledge, his wisp of a body pressed against the glass. Here, the frames rattled if you breathed on them wrong. There was rot in the wood older than Amanda herself. Leo was such an intense child, and so purposeful, that she watched him until she remembered hearing once that glass was just a very slow liquid. Then she ran.

He was so light for four years old. He turned in her

arms and squeezed her neck furiously and whispered, It's *you*.

Leo, she said. That is so dangerous. You could have died.

I was looking at the bird, he said. He pressed a finger to the glass, and she saw, down on the white rocks, some sort of raptor with a short beak. Huge and dangerous even dead.

It fell out of the sky, he said. I was watching the black go blue. And the bird fell. I saw it. Boom. The bad thing, I thought, but actually it's just a bird.

The bad thing? she said, but Leo didn't answer. She said, Leo, you are one eerie mammer jammer.

My mom says that, he said. She says I give her the wet willies. But I need my breakfast now, he said, and wiped his nose on the strap of her sports bra.

Leo bit carefully into his toast and Nutella, watching Amanda. She'd never met a child with beady eyes before. Beadiness arrives after long slow ekes of disappointment, usually in middle age. She had to turn away from him and saw the light spread into the pool and set it aglow.

Are you a kid or a mom? Leo said.

Jesus, Leo, she said. Neither. Yet.

Why not? he said.

She didn't believe in lying to children. This she might

reconsider if she had one. Grant and I've been too poor, she said.

Why? he said.

She shrugged. Student loans. I work with homeless people. His company is getting off the ground. The usual. But we're trying. I may be someone's mom soon. Maybe next year.

So you're not poor anymore? he said.

You practice radical bluntness, I see, she said. We are, yes. But I can't wait forever.

Leo looked at the giraffe tattoo that ran up from her elbow to nibble on her ear. It made him vaguely excited. He looked at the goosebumps between her sports bra and running shorts. My mom says only Americans jog. She says they have no sense of dignity.

Ha! Amanda said. I know your mom from back when her name was Jennifer. She's as American as they come.

As they come? As who comes? Genevieve said from the doorway. So much coming this morning! she said, showing her large white teeth.

Sorry about that, Amanda said, but she didn't mean it.

Genevieve walked lightly across the flagstone floor and kissed her son on his pale cowlick. Her tunic was see-through silk, the bikini beneath black. She wore sunglasses inside.

Hi, Jennifer, Leo said slyly.

Too much wine last night? Amanda said. Was the restaurant worth all of its stars?

But Genevieve was looking at her son. Did you just call me Jennifer? she said.

Aunt Manda told me, he said. And someone *is* coming today. The girl. The one that's taking care of me until we can go home.

Genevieve propped her sunglasses on her crown and made a face. Amanda closed her eyes and said, Jesus, Genevieve. Mina's coming. My niece.

Oh my God, Genevieve said. Oh, that's right. What time's her flight? Three. She did some calculations and groaned and said, Whole day shot to hell.

Because you had some extremely important business, Amanda said. Pilates. Flower arranging. Yet another trip to yet another *cave* to taste yet another champagne. Such a sacrifice to take a few hours to pick up Mina, who's basically my sister, the person who will be watching your child for the rest of the summer for the price of a plane ticket—

I get it, Genevieve said.

—a ticket, Amanda was saying, that Grant and I bought so that we could go out to dinner at least once on our only vacation in four years, instead of babysitting for Leo for a week while you go out.

The women both looked at Leo, flinching.

Whom I love very much, Amanda said. But still.

Do you feel better? Genevieve said. Some people just don't mellow with age, she said to her son.

Leo slid off his stool and went out the veranda doors, down the long slope toward the pool.

If I didn't love you like a sister, I'd throttle the shit out of you, Amanda said.

Her boy gone, Genevieve's smile was, too. The skin of her face was silk that had been clenched in a hand. I guess you have the right to be upset, she said. I've been using you. But you know that food's the only thing that wakes Manfred up and Leo can't go to those restaurants.

Amanda breathed. Her anger was always quick to flare itself out. She came slowly over the distance and hugged her friend, always so tiny, but so skinny these days, her bones as if made of chalk. I'm just frustrated, she said into Genevieve's crown. You know we're mostly fine with it, especially since you're letting us drink all of your champagne.

Genevieve leaned against Amanda and rested for some time there.

Oh, my. Well, hello ladies, Grant said, having come down the stairs silently. His lanky arms suspended him in the doorway, his eyes lovelier for the sleep still in them. So beautiful, her husband, Amanda thought. Scruffy, the light on the flecks of white at his temples. Unfair how men got better-looking as they aged. He'd been a little more beautiful than Amanda when they had met; but maybe he only masked his beauty under all the hemp and idealism then.

When the women stepped apart, Grant said, Even better idea. Let's take it all upstairs, and he winked.

Big fat perv, Amanda said, and kissed him, her hands

briefly in his curls, and went out into the driveway, walking a circle around the dead bird before setting off on a run down the hill toward the village.

Genevieve and Grant listened to Amanda's footsteps until they were gone. Grant smiled. Genevieve smiled. Grant raised an eyebrow and nodded upward toward the room under the eaves. Genevieve bit her bottom lip. She looked down the lawn; Leo was all the way past the pool, in the cherry orchard, huddling over something in the grass. She looked at Grant wryly, and he held out his hand.

She moved toward him, but before they touched, they heard a step heavy on the stairs. Manfred.

Fuck, Grant mouthed.

Later, Genevieve mouthed. She clicked the gas on the stovetop, pulled eggs from the refrigerator. The flush had already faded from her cheeks when she cracked them in the pan.

Grant set the espresso maker on the stove; Manfred entered the room. His hair was silvery and swept back, and he carried himself like a man a foot taller and a hundred pounds lighter.

The old swelling in Genevieve's chest to see him in his crisp white shirt and moccasins. He sat at the scrubbed pine table in its block of sun and lifted his fine face to the warmth like a cat.

Darling, she said. How do you feel today?

I'm having difficulty, he said softly. Things aren't coming back.

LAUREN GROFF

She measured out his pills into her hand and poured sparkling water into a glass. It hasn't been three weeks yet, she said. Last time you got it all back at around three weeks. She handed him the pills, the glass. She pressed her cheek to the top of his head, breathing him in.

Eggs are burning, Grant said.

Then flip them, she said without looking up.

The bees above Leo were loud already. Grass cold with dew. Leo was careful with the twigs. He wouldn't look at the vines beyond; they were too much like columns of men with their arms over one another's shoulders. Beyond were tractors and the Frenchmen in the fields, too far to pluck meaning out of their words: *zhazhazhazhazha*. There was a time before Manda came, and after his father returned from the hospital looking like a boiled potato, when there had been a nice old lady from the village who had cooked their dinners for them. She'd let Leo stay some nights with her when his mother couldn't stop crying. Her pantry had been long and cold and lined with shining jars and tins of cookies. She'd had hens in her yard and a fig tree, and she got cream from her son. That's where he'd go if Manda didn't take him when she left. With the thought, his body buzzed with worry as if also filled with bees. Manda was his beautiful giraffe. He'd set all the rest of them on fire if he could. When he was finished with his work, he went back up the hill. In the kitchen, Grant was drinking coffee and reading a novel, and Leo's father was slowly cutting a plate of eggs to bleed their yellow on a slab of ham. There was yolk on his chin. Leo took the poker and shovel from the great stone hearth. There was a tiny cube of cheese in the corner that Leo looked at for a long time and imagined popping in his mouth, his molars sinking through the hard skin into the soft interior. He resisted. Outside, the falcon was heavier than he imagined it'd be. He had to rest three times even before he passed his mother doing cat pose beside the pool. She always tried to get him to do it with her, but he didn't see the point. Corpse pose was the position he preferred to do himself. In the orchard again, he put the bird on the pile of twigs that he'd built. He stood back, holding his breath. The wind came and the bird's feathers ruffled, and he watched, feeling the miracle about to bloom. But the wind died again and the bird remained stiff on the nest he made for it, and it, like everything, was still dead.

As soon as they were in the car, Amanda felt lighter. She didn't like to think this way, but there was something oppressive about Manfred. A reverse star, sucking in all light.

We may as well get lunch in the city, Genevieve said as they wound through the village.

I can't believe we're going to Paris, Amanda said. She

thought of pâté, of crêpes, neither of which she'd ever had served by an actual French person. Her wet hair filled the car with the scent of rosemary. Leo in the backseat flared it, eyes closed.

You've never been to Paris? Genevieve said. But you were a French major in college.

Those were the years their friendship had gone dark. Genevieve had been shipped up to her fancy New England college, had gone quiet among her new friends. Amanda had been stuck at UF, pretending she hadn't grown up down the street. They reconnected a few years after graduation when Genevieve took a job in Florida, though Sarasota barely qualified.

Never made it to France at all, Amanda said. I had to have three jobs just to survive.

But that's what student loans are for, Genevieve said. When Amanda said nothing, Genevieve sighed and made a circular gesture with her hand and said, Aha. I did it again. Privilege. Sorry.

After a little time, Amanda said, My mom once quit smoking and saved the money so I could go. But my dad found her little stash. You know how it goes with my family.

Sure do. Yikes. How is that hot mess?

Better, Amanda said. Dad got put into a VA home, and Mom's wandering around the house. My brothers lost the forklift business last year, but they're okay. And my sister's in Oregon, we think. Nobody's heard from her in three years.

Even Mina? Genevieve said. You said she was in college. She hasn't heard from her mom in three years?

Even Mina, Amanda said. She's been living in our spare room to save money. It's fantastic to have her around, she's like a beam of light, does all the dishes, takes care of the garden. But then again, I basically raised her, even when I was pretty much a baby myself. You remember. I had to change all those fucking diapers so I couldn't even try out for soccer. Sophie was such a whore.

Genevieve laughed and then saw Leo watching them in the mirror and stopped, blowing her cheeks out. My parents are the same as ever, she said. Marching clenched and seething toward eternity.

Remember that Frost poem we used to say when we were wondering which of our families would kill us first? Amanda said. *Some say the world will end in fire, some say in ice.* Et cetera. I would have given anything for a little ice.

At least you had some joy in your family. At least there was love, Genevieve said.

At least your family never made you bleed, Amanda said. Constantly.

Forgotten from the backseat, Leo's little voice: I thought you were sisters.

God, no! Genevieve said, then looked at Amanda and said, Sorry.

Amanda smiled and said, I wouldn't mind sharing some of your mom's genes. Her pretty face. At the very least, her cheekbones. What I could have done if I'd just had those cheekbones. Ruled the world.

You have your own beauty, Genevieve said.

Privilege speaking, yet again, Amanda said, making the circular gesture with her hand.

Leo thought about this through two whole villages. There was a field full of caravans, kids running and a roil of dogs that made him shiver with longing. Why would Amanda want to look like his mom when Amanda was so very, very lovely? But when he started to ask, the women were already talking about other things.

The sun moved. Manfred moved his chair with it. He thought of nothing, time the consistency of water. Energy was being conserved until there was enough to let it blow bright and blow itself out. He couldn't see it coming yet, but could sense the build. He longed for the aftermath. Silence, nothing. The songbirds were holding their songs; all outside was still. The tall man the women had left behind flittered from place to place without settling. Manfred didn't bother to listen when he spoke. At noon the sun was overhead and the last slip of warmth fled. Manfred was left in the cold. Soon he would stand; he thought of the dinner he would make tonight, planned every bite. His energy was finite, after all, and he must save it. He opened his fingers to find that the pills had dissolved into a paste in his palm, the way they had the day before and the day before.

The women had taken a table in a plaza framed with plane trees. An empty carousel spun. Amanda once saw a mother who had lost her children in a grocery store who had had the same hysterical brightness.

Monoprix? Amanda said. Her first Parisian food and it was from a five-and-dime.

Honey, we only have an hour and the café's not terrible. Also, Leo loves the carousel, Genevieve said.

The backs of Amanda's eyelids felt sanded.

Lunch is on me! Genevieve said.

Well, then: Amanda ordered the lobster salad and a whole bottle of cold white wine. The waitress frowned at her French and answered in English. Genevieve was driving but motioned for a glass for herself.

Leo gazed at the carousel without touching his steak-frites, until Genevieve loosed him with a handful of euros and he ran off. He spoke in each animal's ear until he settled on a flying monkey. The man operating the carousel boosted him up and Leo clung to the monkey's neck and the music began and the monkey moved up and down on its pole. Amanda watched Leo go around three times. He was serious, unsmiling. She ate his fries before they went cold.

I'm sorry this isn't nicer, Genevieve said. You'll have time to eat well before you fly home next week.

I hope so, Amanda said.

Truth is, we're cutting costs a bit, Genevieve said wearily.

Amanda laughed until her eyes were damp. So ludicrous. Where are you cutting costs? she said when she caught her breath. Your fifteen-thousand-square-foot house in Sarasota? The castle in the Alps?

A flicker of irritation over Genevieve's face; but this, too, she quelled. Sarasota is being rented to a rapper for the year, she said. And the castle has been sold.

But. Wait. I thought that was Manfred's family place, Amanda said.

Three centuries, Genevieve said. It couldn't be helped.

Amanda picked up her full glass and drank and drank and put her glass down when it was empty. You really are broke, she said.

No joke, Genevieve said. Bankrupt. Manfred's mania went international this time. The rapper's rent is what's keeping us afloat. What is it they say? It's all about the Benjamins.

That's what they said when we were young. Well, in our twenties. I thought the house where we're staying was yours.

No. Manfred's sister's. The poor one, until about six months ago.

Ha! Amanda said. It was so unexpected, this grief for

her friend. She'd become used to seeing Genevieve as her own dumb daydream. The better her.

Don't cry for me, Genevieve said lightly, squeezing Amanda's arm. We'll be okay.

I'm crying for *me*, Amanda said. I don't even know who to envy anymore.

Genevieve studied her friend, leaned forward, opened her mouth. But whatever was about to emerge withdrew itself, because Leo was running toward them across the plaza, his head down. The carousel had stopped. The air had stilled and there was a sudden silence, like wool packed in the ears. Darling! Genevieve called out, half standing, upsetting the last of the bottle of wine.

And then the blanket covering the sky ripped open, and Leo, still running, vanished in the downpour. Leo! they both shouted. In a moment, the boy appeared on Amanda's side of the table, and he put his cold face on her bare legs. Then there was the blind run through the rain, holding the little boy by the hand between them. They reached the parking garage, a wall of dryness and light. They laughed with relief and turned to look at the curtain of rain a foot beyond them, at the wet dusk that had descended so swiftly in midday.

But as they watched, shivering, there was a great crack and a bolt of light split the plaza wide open and the lightning doubled itself on the wet ground, the carousel in sudden gray scale and all the animals bulge-eyed and fleeing in terror. The others crowded into Amanda, put their faces on her shoulder and her hip. She held them and watched the tumult through the sear of red that faded from her vision. Something in her had risen with the rain, was exulting.

They were still wet when they arrived at the airport. Genevieve's dress was soaked at the shoulders and back, her hair frizzed in a great red pouf. Leo looked molded of wax.

Mina, on the other hand, was fresh even off the plane. Stunning. Red lipstick, high heels, miniskirt, one-shoulder shirt. Earbuds in her ears, accompanied by her own soundtrack. Even in Paris, the men melted from her path as she walked. Amanda watched her approach, her throat thick with pride.

One more year of college, and the world would blow up wherever Mina touched it. Smart, strong, gorgeous, everything. Amanda could hardly believe they were related and found herself saying the silent prayer she said whenever she saw her niece. The girl hugged her aunt hard and long then turned to Leo and Genevieve.

Leo was looking up the long stretch of Mina, his mouth open.

Genevieve said, But you can't be Mina.

I can't? Mina laughed. I am.

Genevieve turned to Amanda, distressed. But I was there when she was born, she said. I was in the hospital with you, I saw the baby before her mother did because Sophie had lost so much blood she was passed out. I left for college when Mina was five. She looked just like your sister. She was fair.

Oh, said Mina, leaning against Amanda. I see. She means I can't be me because I'm black.

Amanda held her laugh until it passed, then said, Her father was apparently African American, Genevieve.

I'm sorry? Genevieve said.

I grew up and everything got darker, Mina said. It happens sometimes. No big deal. Hi, she said, bending to Leo. You must be my very own kiddo. I'm beyond pleased to make your acquaintance, Mr. Leo.

You, he breathed.

We're going to be friends, Mina said.

I'm so sorry. It's just that you're so beautiful, Genevieve said. I can't believe you're all grown up and so gorgeous to boot.

Mina said, You're pretty, too.

Oh, God! The condescension in her voice: Amanda wanted to squeeze her.

Let's get a move on, Amanda said. We have to speed home if we're going to get to the shops down in the village and buy some dinner before they close.

Amanda knew that in the car Genevieve would tell too much about herself, confide to Mina about Manfred's electroshock therapy, about Leo's enuresis, about her own gut issues whenever she ate too much bread. Amanda would sit in the front seat, ostentatiously withholding judgment. In the backseat, Mina and Leo would be playing a silent game of handsies, cementing their alliance. Out in the parking garage, the day felt fresh, newly cold after the rainstorm. As soon as they left the city, the washed fields shone gold and green in the afternoon sun.

t was time. Manfred rose from his chair. Grant nearly choked on his apple. All morning he'd swum in the pool and pretended to work on the website he was designing—the very last he'd ever design, no more jobs lined up—and all afternoon he'd played solitaire on his computer. He'd come to believe that he'd been left alone in the house. The other man had been so still that he had become furniture. It had been easier when Grant believed himself alone. He had all day in silence to defend himself against the thought of Mina: the kiss he'd taken in the laundry room, the chug of machine and smell of softener, the punch so hard he'd had a contusion on his temple for a week afterward. He could be forgiven. It would all be over soon enough, in any event.

The women will be back soon. We should make our preparations, Manfred said, walking out to the Fiat that Grant and Amanda had rented.

Crazy motherfucker, Grant said to himself, but reached for his keys and wallet. He started the car and almost pulled out onto the road but there was a line of tractors heading up the hill homeward. They had to wait for the spindly things to pass. Where are we going? Grant said, watching the tractors trail around the bend.

The village, of course, Manfred said, his hands tightly clenching his knees.

Of course, said Grant.

The bakery was out of boules, so Manfred selected baguettes reluctantly. He bought a napoleon for dessert; he bought a pastel assortment of macarons. Leo loves these, he said to Grant, but before they reached the green-grocer's, he'd already eaten the pistachio and the rose.

He bought eggplants, he bought leeks, he bought en-dives and grapes; he bought butter and cream and crème fraîche, he bought six different cheeses all wrapped in brown paper.

At the wine store, he bought a case of a nice Bour-gogne. We have enough champagne at the house, I think, he said.

Grant thought of the full crates stacked in the corner of the kitchen. I'm not sure, he said.

Manfred looked at Grant's face for the first time, worry passing over his own, then relaxed. Ah, he said. You are joking.

At the butcher's, lurid flesh under glass. Manfred bought sausages, veal, terrine in its slab of fat; he bought thin ham. Grant, who was carrying nearly all the crates and bags, could barely straighten his arms when they reached the car. Manfred looked to the sky and whistled through his front teeth at something he saw there, but Grant didn't pay attention.

We shall have a feast tonight, Manfred said once they'd gotten in and closed the doors.

We shall, Grant said. The little car felt overloaded, starting up the hill.

From behind, from the east, there came a whistling noise, and Grant looked in the rearview mirror to see a wall of water climbing the hill much more swiftly than the car could go. He flipped on the wipers and lights just as the hard rain began to pound on the roof. Grant couldn't see to drive. He pulled into the ditch, leaving two wheels in the road. If anybody sped up the hill behind him, the Fiat would be crushed.

Manfred watched the sheets of water dreamily, and Grant let the silence grow between them. It wasn't unpleasant to sit like this with another man. All at once, Manfred said, his voice almost too soft under the percussive rain, I like your wife.

Grant couldn't think, quite, what to say to this. The silence became edged, and Manfred said with a small smile, More than you do, perhaps.

Oh, no, Grant said. Amanda's great.

Manfred waited, and Grant said, feeling as if he should have more enthusiasm, I mean, she's so kind. And so smart, too. She's the best.

But, Manfred said.

No. No, Grant said. No buts. She is. It's just that I got

into law school in Ann Arbor and she doesn't know yet. That I'm going.

He did not say that Amanda would never go with him, couldn't leave her insane battered mother behind in Florida. Or that as soon as he realized he would go up to Michigan alone, leaving behind the incontinent old cat he hated, the shitty linoleum, the scrimping, the buying of bad toilet paper with coupons, Florida and its soul-sucking heat, he felt light. A week ago, when they drove up to the ancient stone house framed in all of those grapevines, he knew that this was what he wanted: history, old linen and crystal, Europe, beauty. Amanda didn't fit. By now, she was so far away from him, he could barely see her.

He felt a pain somewhere around his lungs; dismay. What he did say was so small but still a betrayal of its kind.

I'm waiting for the right time to tell Amanda, so don't say anything, please, he said.

Manfred's hands held each other. His face was blank. He was watching the wall of rain out the windshield.

Grant took a breath and said, I'm sorry. You weren't even listening.

Manfred flicked his eyes in Grant's direction. So leave. What does it matter. Everyone leaves. It is not the big story in the end.

Like that, the stone that had pressed on his shoulders had been lifted. Grant began to smile. Grade-A wisdom there, buddy, he said. Lightning sizzled far off in the sky. They watched.

Except there is one thing you must tell me, Manfred said suddenly. Who is this Ann Arbor woman? And, when Grant looked startled, Manfred gave another small smile and said, That was also a joke, and Grant laughed in relief and said, Seriously, please don't tell Amanda, and Manfred inclined his head.

Grant felt uncomfortably intimate with Manfred so close in the tiny car. There had been something he'd wanted to say since Genevieve's wedding in Sarasota ten years ago, during what was in retrospect clearly a manic swing of Manfred's pendulum. There had been peacocks running around the gardens; the guest favors were silver bowls. Grant had watched, making little comments about the excess that Amanda lobbed back with extra bitter spin. He saw things differently now.

Forgive me for saying this, Grant said. But sometimes you even look like an Austrian count. You have a certain nobility to you.

But I am only a Swiss baron, Manfred said. It means nothing.

It means something to me, Grant said.

It would, Manfred said. You are very American. You are all secretly royalists.

In the distance, the clouds cracked and slabs of light fell to the ground. Manfred sighed. He said, We have had a pleasant talk. But I believe you may drive.

Grant turned the car on and pushed up the hill, home.

The women gave out little yodels of surprise when they arrived to find the men in the kitchen in aprons, chopping vegetables. The men looked at Mina when she came out of the car, and Leo felt power turning and beginning to flow in her direction, like the stream at the bottom of the hillside when he shifted rocks in its bed. Outside smelled like rich earth, like cows. Manfred had poured them all champagne and brought the flutes out on a platter, and they drank it on the wet white gravel, looking at the way the vines sparked with late light, the green and purple tinge to the edge of sky. *To Mina,* they all said. Even Leo got an inch of champagne, which he had always loved like cola. He downed it. His mother was watching his father carefully over her drink, and it was true his father had a dangerous pink in his cheeks. Badness moved in Leo. He stole into the kitchen, now dim with dusk, and to the fireplace, the small ceramic box that had *Allumettes* written on it, or so Manda had said a few days earlier with her shy French. Leo had to wait for Grant to come in, bouncing Mina's suitcases up the stairs. His mother and Mina followed behind, his mother explaining the wonky shower, Leo's schedule, how Leo couldn't swim yet so everyone had to be careful with the pool. Leo's father gravely handed him a purple macaron and turned back to cook, and Leo put the sweet thing up the chimney for the pigeons to eat. He hated macarons. He came out on the grass, past the pool, down into the cool orchard with its sticky smell. It appeared that the falcon had grown while he'd gone. It was huge with the shadows that had fallen on it. He stood over the bird on its nest and said words in German, then English, then French. He made some magic words up and said them. In one of his father's old books, back at home in the castle in the Alps, there had been a drawing of an old bird set aflame, and in the next illustration, it turned into a glorious new bird. Leo thought with longing of his own bed there, his own books and his own toys, and the mountain in his window when he awoke. He struck the match on a stone. The flame sizzled then took. The sticks were wet but not right under the bird, and those dry twigs caught just before the flame touched his hand. The bird's feathers, burning, let off a reek that he hadn't foreseen. He stepped back, crouching on his heels, to watch. Black roil of smoke. When he looked up again, it was much later; shadows around him deepened. The bird was a charred, ugly thing now, half feathered, half flesh. The fire had gone out entirely; there was no more red in the embers. Someone was calling for him, *Leo, Leo!* He stood and ran up the hill, feeling weariness in his legs and all along the back of his neck. It was Mina calling for him with the sunset bright in her hair, with another glass of champagne shining in her hand. Someone is burning something awful, she said, sniffing. An orange-faced boy rode by on a tractor that looked like a leggy animal; he stood up and shouted something gleeful that neither of them caught over the noise. Mina waved, smiled with her teeth. She looked at Leo's dirty face, his dirty hands. She said, laughing, Wash yourself, eat your dinner fast, and I'll give you a bath and put you to bed. His heart could hardly bear all that he was feeling. It was either expanding to the sky or contracting to a pin, hard to say. Leo, his mother called, come give me a kiss. *Die,* he thought, but kissed her anyway on her soft and powdery cheek. He kissed Manda up the giraffe's neck on her neck, and she blushed and laughed. His father he would not. Let the boy be, his father murmured to his mother. The gleam on Mina's legs up the stairs. He would eat her if he could. He let her wash him with warm water and she put him in clean pajamas and he petted her soft cheek and smelled her while she sang him to sleep.

It was chilly outside on the veranda. Amanda wore a fleece, Genevieve wore a brocaded shawl. They waited for the food to cook and ate terrine on baguettes and drank champagne, listening on the monitor to Leo's little piping voice and Mina's gravelly one answering him. There was light coming from the kitchen and on the table one candle in a pewter candlestick that looked ancient. Manfred had put on *Peter and the Wolf*, which was Leo's CD, but all of the other music in the house was his sister's and all of it was 1990s grunge. There was some kind of newborn glitter in Manfred's eyes that Amanda was having a difficult time looking at directly. Something had shifted between Grant and Manfred; there was a humming line between them there had never been before.

Yesterday, Manfred said suddenly, I poisoned the rats in the kitchen. I forgot to say. Do not eat the cheese you will find in the corners.

Poor little rats, said Genevieve. I wish you had told me. I would have found a humane trap somewhere. It's an awful thing to die of thirst. She pulled the shawl tighter to her.

Oh! That explains the falcon, Amanda said. The others looked at her.

Leo saw a falcon fall dead out of the sky this morning, she said. It was huge. It was in the driveway. I don't know how you all missed it. I bet it ate a poisoned rat and croaked in midair.

No, Genevieve said, too quickly.

It seems likely, doesn't it, Manfred said. Oh, dear. It is terrible luck to kill a raptor. It signifies the end of days.

I mean, the thing probably just had a heart attack, Amanda said, but rested her head on her husband's shoulder, and it took him a moment to slide his chair over and put his arm around her.

The wind restrained itself, the treetops shushed. The moon came from behind a cloud and looked at itself in the pool.

Now Mina was singing in the monitor, and Amanda said, Listen! "Au Clair de la Lune." She sang along for a stanza, then had to stop.

Why are you crying, silly? Genevieve said gently, touching Amanda's hair. Twice in a day and you never used to cry. I once saw all four of your big old brothers sitting on you, one of them bouncing on your head, and you didn't cry. You just fought like a wild thing.

Hormones, I think, Amanda said. I don't know. It's just that all those nights when Sophie would go out and leave Mina at our house, I would sing this to her until she went to sleep. For hours and hours. Everybody would be screaming downstairs, just awful things, and once in a while the cops would show up, and there would be flashing lights in the window. But in my bed, there'd be this sweet beautiful baby girl sucking her thumb and saying, Sing it again. And so I'd sing it again and again and again, and it was all I could do.

They listened to Mina's beautiful, raspy voice over the monitor . . . *Il dit à son tour— Ouvrez votre porte, pour le dieu d'amour.*

Well, thank God for Madame Dupont, Genevieve said. Forcing us to learn it in seventh grade. She made us sing at school assembly, remember? I wanted to die.

Nobody looked at Manfred; they studied the knives, the bread. The moment passed.

Grant said, What's she saying?

There were tears in his eyes, Amanda saw; she squeezed

the back of his neck. She was moved. It had been so long since she had seen the side of him that would weep during movies about dolphin harvests. A different Grant had grown up over him, a harder one.

Manfred didn't seem inclined to translate. Amanda listened for a minute to gather herself. It's a story, she said. Harlequin wants to write a letter, but he doesn't have a pen and his fire went out, and so he goes to his buddy Pierrot to borrow them. But Pierrot is in bed and won't open the door, and he tells Harlequin to go to the neighbor's to ask because he can hear someone making a fire in her kitchen. And then Harlequin and the neighbor fall in love. It's silly, she said. A pretty lullaby.

But Manfred was looking at her from the shadows. He leaned forward. Dear Amanda, he said. The world must be hard for you. All substance, no nuance. Harlequin is on the prowl. He wants sex, *pour l'amour de Dieu*. When Pierrot turns him away, he goes to the neighbor to *battre le briquet*. Double entendre, you see. He is, in the end, fucking the neighbor.

Genevieve sat back slowly in the darkness.

Manfred smiled at Amanda, and there was a strange new electricity in the air; there was something here, announcing itself to Amanda, in the very back of her head. It had almost arrived, the understanding; it was almost here. She held her breath to let it step shyly forward into the light.

———

Mina watched the couples from the doorway, feeling as if she were still flying over the Atlantic, the ground distant and swift beneath. Nobody was speaking; they were not looking at one another. Something had soured since she'd left them half an hour ago. She had come from a house of conflict. She knew just by looking that there would be an argument breaking out in a moment and that it would be bad.

She took a step out to distract them. She started singing. She didn't have a good voice, but she was loud and her singing sometimes would disarm a fight at home. The other four snapped their eyes up at her. She felt herself expanding into her body as she always did when she was watched. She was new tonight, strange. The champagne was all she'd consumed since leaving Orlando, and it made her feel languorous, like a cat.

Sometime between arrival and now, she'd finally decided what she'd been mulling over for the past few days; and now what she knew and what they didn't filled her with a secret lift of joy. Internal helium. She wouldn't board the plane at the end of the summer. School was so gray and useless compared to what waited for her in Paris, her life on hold in that hot place where she'd lived her childhood out. Florida. Well. She was finished with all of that. A whole continent in the past. She would go toward the glamour. She was only twenty-one. She was beautiful. She could do whatever she wanted to. She felt herself on the exhilarating upward climb in her life. As she walked toward them, she saw how these people at the table had stopped climbing, how they were teetering on the precipice (even Amanda, poor tired Amanda). That Manfred man was already hurtling down. He was a mere breath from the rocks.

This sky huge with stars. Glorious, Mina thought, as she walked toward them. The cold in the air, the smell of cherries wafting up from the trees, the veal and endives cooking in the kitchen, the pool with its own moon, the stone house, the vines, the country full of velvet-eyed Frenchmen. Even the flicks of candlelight on those angry faces at the table was romantic. Everything was beautiful. Anything was possible. The whole world had been split open like a peach. And these poor people, these poor fucking people. Were they too old to see it? All they had to do was reach out and pluck it and raise it to their lips, and they would taste it, too.

SALVADOR

The apartment Helena rented in Salvador had high ceilings, marble floors, vast windows. It always looked cool, even when the blaze of a Brazilian summer crept inside in the late afternoon. If she leaned from her balcony, she could see the former convent that curved around her street's cul-de-sac; she could see over the red tile roofs of the buildings across the way to where the harbor opened into ocean. She was so close she could smell faint littoral rot and taste the salt on the wind. For the first few mornings, she took her coffee out to the balcony in her cotton nightgown and watched the water sweeping greenly toward the horizon, ocean and sky faltering into haze where they met.

One morning when she was on the balcony enjoying the nightgown's graze against her ankles and the sharp summer sunlight, she looked down to find the shopkeeper from the grocery across the street looking up at her. He had a broom in his hand, but he wasn't sweeping.

His round, dark face, always glistening as if just brushed with hot butter, was turned up toward her. His lips were open, and his tongue was pressing rapidly into the gap between his two front teeth, all pink and wet and lewd.

She went inside and shut the glass door hard and put her coffee cup down very carefully on the glass dining table. She felt ill. She went into the bedroom to look at herself. The same light that fell across the balcony was slicing through the windows in her room, and she stood in the pool of it to see what he'd seen. In the mirror, all was apparent, literally: she could see her entire body—legs, dark pubis, round brown nipples—as if her night-gown were only a pale shadow of her own skin. Helena thought of the man's view from below, the pink soles of her feet pressing through the keyhole shapes in the balcony's floor, the taper of her legs to her bust, her head topped with dyed yellow hair brazenly unbrushed.

Jesus Christ, I look like a whore, she said. Helena laughed at herself, and the laugh broke the spell, and she showered and dressed and went out for the day. As she passed the grocery, she stared straight ahead, unwilling to give the shopkeeper the satisfaction of seeing her look into the dark recesses of his store.

Helena was in that viscous pool of years in her late thirties when she could feel her beauty slowly departing from her. She had been lovely at one time, which slid into pretty, which slid into attractive, and now, if she didn't do something major to halt the slide, she'd end up at handsomely middle-aged, which was no place at all to be. She was the youngest daughter of a mother too perennially ill to live alone, and being the youngest and unmarried at the time of her mother's first bloom of illness, Helena was the one to fall into the caretaking role. For the most part, her life with her mother was calm, even good, with whist and euchre and jigsaw puzzles and television programs, with all that church on Sundays, ferociously antedated, in Latin, with veils. Helena herself believed in no god but the one that moved in her mother's face when she genuflected on the velvet and forgot how ill she was.

She was, on the whole, fine with the arrangement, fine with being her mother's keeper. It had to be said, however, that love was impossible with a sick and saintly mother patiently bearing her insomnia in the room next door. There was no question of dating, either, because her mother needed help every few hours to go to the bathroom or remember a pill or a shot, for a lap to lay her head in and a hand to wipe away the moisture at her temples.

Helena's sisters felt horribly guilty watching their beautiful sister fade in such dutiful servitude, and so they gave Helena a good chunk of money every year and came to spend two weeks apiece caring for their mother in Helena's stead. For a month a year, Helena had the freedom and funds to spend her time wherever she wanted. She mostly chose to visit quiet places bedaubed with romance—Verona, Yalta, Davos, Aracataca—and to stretch her cash reserves, she rented a furnished apartment and ate only dinners out. She'd spend the days in museums and coffee shops and botanical gardens, and at night, more often than not, she'd come giggling back home with her pumps in one hand, exchanging sloppy kisses with a stranger in the elevator.

She had no trouble finding men, even if it was undeniable that her looks were slipping. If, at the restaurant she chose, a man didn't approach her, she went to the bar of a nice hotel. If nothing happened at the bar, she went to a nightclub and brought home drunk boys half her age. She preferred blond businessmen above all, but there was a different and sometimes more intense pleasure in these young men, natives of the places she visited, something delicious in the way their languages slid past each other, only barely touching.

Men were not as disciplined or as smart as women, she thought; men almost always took what they were offered, their appetites too crude and raw to put up much resistance. They were like children, gobbling down their candy all at once, with no thought about the consequences of their greed. She and her visitors often kept the neighbors awake, but the neighbors rarely complained; when they met her in the hallway, they usually became confused by the neat and elegant gray dresses Helena wore, her severe tight bun, her pale and haughty face. It felt wrong, somehow, to make such an embarrassing complaint of a woman whose posture was so very correct.

After her month of slaking her thirsts, Helena found she was almost eager to return to the close, doily-riddled apartment and her mother's half-swallowed cries of pain in the night.

A week after the shopkeeper had seen her in all her glory, two weeks into her stay in Salvador, she came home early one morning with one of her boys. She'd met a group of flight attendants at a bar, and their lone man was clearly uninterested in her, or perhaps in women in general, and so she'd gone along with the giddy bunch to a local nightclub. There they were out of place among the gorgeous young creatures with their barely-there clothing, their feline sleekness. The flight attendants eventually vanished, and Helena was left dancing with a tall, very dark-skinned man of eighteen or so. Though his English was limited to the rap lyrics he mouthed to the music, she managed to convey what she wanted to do to him. He grinned beautifully. They rode his scooter to her part of the city, Helena pressing her pelvis against him as they rode, touching him, and he went so fast he nearly lost control when they hit the cobblestones. They laughed with relief and something richer when he turned the bike off, and they slid down and, hushing each other, went together through the wrought-iron fence. She pulled the gate closed and glanced out into the street as it clanged. She was startled to see the moon-faced shopkeeper. He was in a crouch, about to pull up the metal gate protecting his storefront. He was watching her. She felt the smile fall off her face as he gave an imperceptible shake of his head and turned his back. She had a sudden urge to call out to him, something desperate and true, about the long, dry years spent in the wilderness of her mother's illness, but the boy drew her away by the waist, his voice warm and sibilant and nonsensical in her ear, and when she looked back, the shopkeeper had turned away.

Helena woke in the mid-morning to find the boy gone. In the kitchen, she discovered a plate he'd left with a smiley face drawn on it in hot sauce, and she set it in the sink and watched as the face dissolved under a stream of water. She spent the morning slowly caring for her body, taking a long bubble bath and exfoliating and depilating, filing and polishing, seeing elaborately to her hair. The gnawing feeling she'd woken to hadn't gone away, and so she put on her primmest outfit, a long black dress and sturdy walking sandals. She hesitated and threw a shawl around her shoulders to give an even fustier impression. She hadn't, as yet, bought anything from the grocery across the street—the owner of the apartment had warned her in his letter that the prices at the clean chain grocery three blocks northward were half what the

local shop's were—but she needed some bananas and pa-
payas and coffee and bread, and she gathered her courage
to face the shopkeeper.

The store smelled strongly of fruit on the cusp of rot,
and the shelves were packed, the rows tight. Two people
with baskets could have hardly slid by each other. There
was nobody else in the store, she was relieved to see, save
the shopkeeper and a friend of his who had been chatting
by the register until she came in. She gave them a small
nod, and they nodded back, both unsmiling.

She browsed for a while, until the men began to speak
again in a low tone. Back by the toilet paper and festive
paper napkins there was a little narrow doorway in the
wall, which was empty when she first looked past it. When
she looked again, though, she saw a small foot, then a
hand, a dark head. When the whole person came into the
light, she was either a very short woman or a young girl.
Helena assumed she was indigenous, brown-skinned and
broad-cheekboned, then wondered if she was the shopkeeper's daughter, though she had assumed the moment
she saw him that the shopkeeper was black; he was
only slightly lighter than the boy from last night. But Brazil was so confusing this way, Salvador especially so, with
its slave-trade blight of long ago: you never could tell exactly where people belonged. She had been surprised to
find that this city upset some deep Northern Hemisphere
sense of order that she didn't know she treasured.

The shopkeeper saw the girl or woman and said

something in a harsh voice, and by the swift fear Helena saw on her face, the way her shoulders dropped subserviently, and the speed with which she vanished from sight, Helena thought there was something wrong here. She didn't know what to do; she had to swiftly rest her head against the cool metal of the shelves to pull herself together. When she took her purchases up to the shopkeeper, her hands were trembling and she could barely look at him, getting only an impression of shortness and powerful shoulders. She fixed on a small tin statuette in the window above his head, a woman knee-deep in sharp-looking waves. Yemanjá, she remembered from the marketplace, goddess of the sea. The man pointed at the numbers on the register with a blunt finger. Helena paid the money to Yemanjá, not to him.

By the time he put her purchases in a plastic sack, she was able to look him full in the face, saying silently, *You are a bad man and I am watching.* For the rest of the day, she fretted over the girl, wondering if she needed rescuing. Still, she savored the way the shopkeeper had flinched under her eyes.

For three days, Helena dressed with ostentatious primness and made small purchases at the grocer's, but the shopkeeper never greeted her and she never saw the girl or woman again. Helena's ardor had cooled by the third day, and she began to wonder if the girl wasn't simply the man's wife or girlfriend or stock person, a person to whom it was a wrong but not a crime to speak to in such a way. She began to feel a chill of guilt that she had jumped to such conclusions—what an arrogant, American thing to do!—and to avoid the whole marshy emotional terrain, she began making her purchases at the chain again.

On a trip back from the other store, her milk and eggs swinging in a bag by her hip, she saw the shopkeeper out in front of his store, and he looked first at her bag, and something folded in his face, and he gave her a not-unfriendly wave, and she, confused, pretended to not see him.

Upstairs in her apartment, she fretted. Was she never to walk out of her house without being swamped with bad feelings? Was the shopkeeper going to ruin her entire vacation? She made herself a fruit salad and sat vengefully on her balcony to eat it. A great thick cloud had formed, and the wind had risen, and when she finished, she stood to take a look at the ocean. She watched as a distant sheet of water descended from the black clouds and sped toward her, drawing a swift curtain over the cruise ships outside the harbor, then the fishing boats motoring in, then the harbor itself, then the church steeple. When it hit the red rooftop across the street, she stepped inside and shut her glass door a breath before the storm smacked loudly at her, as if raging that she was still dry and safe when all the rest of the world was vulnerable.

The storm against the many windows was terrifically loud, and for a full day, Helena was stuck in the apartment, unable to go out to her museums or films or restaurants and bars and nightclubs. She read all of her books and wrote letters to her sisters and mother, telling them of this strange, dreamy town with its pastels and hills and wandering bands of drummer girls who danced under the streetlights and played ferociously in the former slave market filled with textiles and handicrafts. She wrote of the first man she had met there, though she stretched the truth far out of shape, taking what was simply a jet-lagged hour or so and implying a love affair, as she always did in her letters during her months at large. Her mother was a romantic, and her sisters, stuck in their happy marriages, only pretended to censure her entanglements, tsking and gorging themselves for a full year on Helena's hints and subtexts. She wrote of visiting the Church of Nosso Senhor do Bonfim, translating it as Our Lord of Happy Endings, knowing her mother would hear the sonorous Portuguese and imagine a dark-skinned Jesus on a cross, that her sisters would get the joke and laugh behind their hands.

When a kind of night fell over the afternoon, she felt desperate and tied a plastic shopping bag over her head and wore the only trench coat she'd brought, because it was supposed to be summer in the Southern Hemisphere, after all. She ran, holding her shoes, to the convent-cum-fine-hotel at the end of the street. At the very last second, the bellhop opened the door for her and she burst into the lobby, laughing and shaking the water from her yellow hair and untying the plastic bag from her head in a vast gold-framed mirror. This was much better, she thought as she surveyed the hotel with its jungle of plants and woodwork, then checked her hair and makeup. She was flushed and very pretty. She slid on her shoes, and the bellhop gave her a little applause and gestured to the fire.

But she shook her head and went over to the bar, which was normally too expensive for her. The storm had kept her in the night before and she couldn't give a fig for budget; she needed to make up for lost time and her sort of businessman frequented this kind of hotel. She caught her breath and sipped her Scotch and watched the display behind the bar, blue-lit bubbles in some kind of oil, rising with preposterous slowness.

There was a pair of American men who smiled back at her, but who were joined instantly by their wives in print dresses. She winked at an old fellow who looked alarmed and tottered away; she slowly put on a coat of lipstick in the direction of a Japanese businessman who had eyes only for his computer. There was no one else, and the bartender was a woman. Helena ordered a hamburger with a luxurious heap of fried onions and gorgonzola on it, and ate it slowly in neat bites, watching the doorway where nobody came in.

The lights flickered and went out, but there were candles on the table in a soft constellation. She watched the bartender light more until the room was again twilit.

She felt full of frantic energy by the time she had finished her food, but from the deafening sound of the rain outside, it was going to be a dud night. Nobody in his right mind would go out in such weather. Reluctantly, in the light from the fire and the scattered candles, Helena tied the shopping bag over her head again and slid on her unpleasantly soaked trench coat. At the door, however, the bellhop shook his head and said, No, no, miss! and waved his arms.

I know it's storming, but my apartment is literally fifty feet away, she said, touched by his distress. She tried to show him through the glass, but the rain was so thick and the night so dark that the world melted away a foot from where they stood. She grinned at him—he was cute, big-eared; in such a pinch he would do—but he only turned toward the reception desk and called out something. A woman rushed over. She was tall, a German Brazilian, Helena thought, with hazel eyes and long streaked hair, and Helena felt a warm burst of hatred rise in her, for the woman was more beautiful than Helena had ever been, even in her prime.

Miss, the woman said. We cannot let you go. It is a tremendous rain. With winds. What is the word?

Not a hurricane, Helena said. There are no hurricanes in the South Atlantic. She knew this because her mother had fretted, and Helena had found the entry on Brazil in the old set of encyclopedias to put her mind at ease.

Well, the woman said, shrugging. But even if it is only a storm, you must stay.

Helena explained again about the apartment, so few feet away, and suggested that she bring the bellhop with her, glancing under her lashes at him, wondering if he'd take the hint. But he took a step backward, and there was such terror on his pale little face that she laughed. I'll be all right, she said.

Stay, the woman said. I will give you a room for half price.

Helena felt herself flushing, but said, Which is?

The woman said a price that was the cost of the entire month of her apartment's rent. Too much, Helena said.

Quarter price, the woman said in distress. I am not authorized to go more low.

Thank you, Helena said. I'll be all right. She took off her shoes, snatched open the door, marched out, and immediately knew that she had made a mistake.

The wind carried her breath from her mouth, the rain pounded into her eyes, and Helena stepped back until she felt the hotel's stucco under her hand. She couldn't see the doorway or the rug she had just been standing on, and she was able to breathe only when she made a windbreak of the crook of her elbow. She was not one to go back, though, not ever. Her place was a few steps away; it had taken her a minute, at most, to run here barefoot a few hours earlier. She dropped her shoes and felt her way painstakingly over the curve of the old convent to the wrought-iron fence around the courtyard. Here, it was slightly easier because she pulled herself hand over hand like a sailor up a mast, until she reached the next stucco texture, the next building.

By the time she got to this building's doorway, she was weeping. She stopped and pressed her body against the glass and tried the door, but it was either locked or the wind was holding it shut. She breathed for a while in the lee of a mailbox until she stopped crying, and wiped her swollen eyes, and started out again. Stupid woman, she said to herself. Stupid, foolish, terrible woman. You deserve what you get.

She inched forward. There were three more doors, she thought, before her own wrought-iron gate that swung inward, that the wind would whip open as soon as she tried it, and pull her inside the courtyard, home. Or maybe four doors; she couldn't quite remember, and she couldn't believe she hadn't paid much attention before now.

But before she was even to the third door, she tripped over something and went sprawling and felt the skin of her knee open painfully. She curled into a ball to gather her strength and lay there, crying with anger and exhaustion. She was alone and she conceded to her aloneness, she would always be alone, she would always be in these puddles that grew even as she lay in them. For a very long time, she lay there, and it wasn't terrible, despite the wind and rain upon her. It was only blank.

Suddenly, something rushed out of the storm, something seized her wrist, and she felt herself being pulled bodily over the cobblestones, her limbs cracking against the hard ground. And then there was the absence of, first, the wind in her face, then the driving rain; and she opened her eyes to darkness. She was so grateful to be breathing that she didn't wonder where she was until her breath calmed and she hushed the whimper she had just heard rising from her chest and she listened to a harsh metal clang that muffled the storm even more, then a pounding that was the wind angry to be left outside. She pulled herself painfully up and drew her legs in, the cut on her leg smarting terribly, and leaned against whatever was behind her, so soft and covered in plastic. She felt with her hands and knew she was leaning on wrapped paper towels, and only then did her dulled mind grasp that she was in the grocer's. He, of all humans on the planet, had saved her. Now the smell of the place rose to her, the sour half-rot and flour. She heard him shoving something heavy against the door.

A flicker of something ugly began to stir in her, and she pushed herself farther against the paper towels, up onto the shelf, letting the displaced rolls pad onto the floor. She was shivering, and she put the collar of her dress between her teeth to keep them from chattering. The place was dark, the only light from a distant red flickering of something electrical, which illuminated nothing.

Helena hoped for the girl or woman she'd seen on her first visit to be here. She longed for the little body to come close to hers, to hold her hand and warm her, but she listened so acutely she could hear that there was nobody in the store but them, she and this man; their breathing was the only breathing. She forced herself to listen to him, his heavy shoes shuffling closer to where she was sitting. It was maybe an accident that he kicked her calf when he drew near; she couldn't tell what he could see. She held her breath, but he knew every inch of the store, of course, and stepped even closer. She could smell him, a particular stink of feet and armpits and denim that has been worn to grease.

He said nothing, just stood over her for a long time. He gave another shuffle closer and the fabric of his jeans brushed her face and she was glad for the dress in her mouth or she would have shouted.

He said something in his gruff voice, but she didn't understand and didn't bother to respond. She tried to keep her breathing light and unobtrusive, but her stomach, so upset by her struggle and the heavy food, gave a gurgle, and he laughed unpleasantly.

The shopkeeper moved away then, and she felt the

tension fall out of her shoulders. She could hear him rummaging, then the double kiss of a refrigerator opening then closing across the room. She thought wildly of running now but knew she couldn't get the metal door up in this wind, and she was fairly sure there was no back way out of the store. And, as bad as he might be, she had been in the storm outside, and she wasn't sure, but she thought it must be worse.

The man came back. Instead of standing, he sank down opposite to where she was, and she felt a sharp and sudden pain on her throat. But then the pain translated to cold, and she knew that he was holding out a glass bottle to her, and she took it in her hand. On her cheek, then, there was another feel, a slick plastic, and the man said, *Biscoitos,* and she took the package of cookies in her other hand and ate one to be polite. *Obrigado,* she whispered, but he said nothing back.

The drink was beer. She clung to the heft of the bottle in her hand. Though he far outpowered her, he had at least given her a weapon. She drank sparingly to make the weight of the bottle last. Across the dark gulf of the aisle, his gulps were thick and loud, and he must have brought more beer for himself because every so often she heard a clink of an empty bottle on the concrete floor and a hiss of a new beer being opened and the chime of the cap falling to the floor. The storm roared outside steadily, and her feet on the floor began to be tickled, then lapped, by water. The storm was coming in.

Worse than being in the storm was not knowing what the storm was doing. The evidence of it was everywhere: in the cold water up to her rear on her little shelf, in the blast of wind, the rattle of the building, and the sounds of distant crashes, boats, most probably, smashing into the shore. She wondered about fires blazing through the rickety old structures of this part of town, and what would be left in the morning. If she survived this night, this hulk of a man across from her in the darkness, she could close her eyes on the taxi ride to the airport, she could get on a plane, she could soar over the wreckage until the plane landed, her mother in a wheelchair beaming at her from the bottom of the escalator in baggage claim. It would not be her mess to clean up. She was a visitor only; she could be absolved. But this was cold comfort, barely any at all. The end of the storm was unreal, and she was beyond tired. The hours of waiting in the dark here, the years of waiting in the darkness at home, were too much; they overcame her in waves of exhaustion. There was no telling how fast the water would rise. It didn't matter: the man was already here. And Helena waited for his sudden lunge, his powerful body that her own thin one couldn't resist for long.

There was a pop outside, and the man's bulk came

closer, and he said something gruff, and she cringed, but he didn't touch her.

She was lulled by the darkness, the man's immobility save for his drinking. It must be morning by now, at least. Her fear had dulled, and her thoughts were thick with sleep. She rested her head against the towels in their packages and shifted so the cramp in her rear was soothed, and shut her eyes, as if she could make the dark any darker and push the storm and the man farther from her.

The shopkeeper stood three times, there was the kiss of the refrigerator three times, he sloshed back and groaned to the floor opposite her three times. The third time, she was nearly asleep when he leaned over and put his hand on her ankle. He had been holding a beer, and his skin on hers was shockingly cold.

She had feared this for so long, it seemed, that when it was here, it was almost a relief. She felt her anger blaze alive, and she jerked her leg away, but his hand found her ankle again and clamped down to the point of pain, then beyond. She gave an involuntary cry, and he laughed, as if to say that wasn't even close to the limit of his strength, and she bit her lip until it bled, and he loosened his hand again.

She thought of her mother, at home in Miami, where there was only dry sun outside, the crucifix in the shadows above the bed; she thought of the small tin *orixá*, the goddess of the sea, calm above the register in the dark. She found herself praying, not knowing if she was praying to her mother or to either of the gods, or a mixture of all three, but in truth it didn't matter to whom the words were addressed because the act without direction was all she could do.

The shopkeeper removed his hand only to fetch more beer or food from the shelves. He crunched and breathed heavily and smacked his lips, and she remembered how he had tongued the gap between his teeth that day he gazed up at her on her balcony, how pink and pulsing and obscene it was. When he returned, he put his hand on her leg again, each time higher on her calf. The gate rattled with less desperation now; the wind appeared to have died down a little. When he reached her knee, he felt the raw wet mouth of the wound there, and despite herself, she pulled in a hissing breath, and this shook something from him.

He ran his finger over the edges of the wound. Every once in a while, the finger would dart forward and touch inside the cut, and she would gasp, and he would laugh. He began to talk. He was beyond drunk, this was clear, and his tongue was thick and his words were strange, and she was sure she would never have understood his Portuguese even if she spoke the language.

She felt sick with anticipated pain. She clutched herself, waiting, and found her brain transliterating surreally, the long strands of language broken into short strands, swept into a semblance of rhythm. She took comfort in the images that rose in the darkness before her. *Bull's blood zucchini flowerstar,* she imagined he said. *Cinema collation of strange mad zebras.*

She listened. His words thickened. His hand fell back away from her knee, down her calf. Outside, she heard the wind through leaves—there were still trees, then, and the trees still had leaves—and the occasional plink of rain against metal. It could be the eye of the storm, she told herself; and if it was, she would have to bear the intensification of wind again, this man's heavy presence, and she knew what would happen if she had to wait with him once more through the terrible roar outside. She would not be able to be still enough for him to forget her. But at last, the shopkeeper fell silent and a whistling started up in his nose and she understood that he was asleep.

In tiny increments, she extracted her body from under his hand. She stood from the puddle on the concrete where she was sitting and moved, stiff and cold, toward where she remembered the door to be. She had to put down the beer bottle that she had clutched all night to move a shelf out of the way and lift the lock. In a burst of strength, she ripped the gate up and away from the ground.

The day dazzled with sun. Steam rose from the street,

a clean sheet of liquid light covering the cobblestones, a wet skin glittering on the buildings. Gold drops fell from the treelimbs, and a cool gentle wind swept the hair from her face. Her leg was caked with blood, the wound livid, her body racked in the joints. She didn't care.

Behind her, the shopkeeper shifted to his feet, bottles ringing on the wet floor as he struggled. She turned, ready to shout, but he was gazing beyond her into the outside. The reflection from the street pushed into the dark of the store, made his round and greasy face shine with moving sunlight. He held on to the shelf before him, and she saw his fear, different and subtler than hers, rise from him and move deeper into the shadows of the room. The shop-keeper tilted his head and closed his eyes, and soon he said, *Campainhas,* and this was a thing she understood, because she also heard the churchbells ringing into the morning. She said, Yes. He looked at her as if surprised to find her there; he had forgotten her; she was merely the postscript to his tempestuous night. She was a mere visi-tor. She was nothing. Helena reached over to the tin *orixá* above the cash register and found it to be sharper and lighter than she had imagined it, a thought turned to matter, an idea that fit in the palm of her hand.

For a long while, she stood in the doorway, listening to the bells, happy for them; but they went on and on, and she began to listen for them to stop. Each peal, she was sure, would be the last. The bright sound would dissolve back into the sea-touched wind, and the ordinary noises of Salvador would rise to take the bells' place, the calling voices, a scooter, a dog barking, a drum; and Helena would be freed to move forward, outward, up. But each note disintegrated and was followed by another and then another, and she felt stuck where she stood, a wild feeling rising in her. Her body grew unbearably tense; her heart began to beat so fast it felt as if it were winged.

And then she saw, plain as the street before her, her mother in her bedroom at home, pale among her pillows. Helena could not tell if she was alive or dead. She was so peaceful, so very still. The Miami sun fingered the edges of the blinds. The birds filled the loquat tree just outside the window, the tree her mother had planted herself before Helena was born, the fruit already rotten, the birds already drunk on the fruit, wildly singing.

Helena's hands flew out to stop the vision, and the nail of her index finger began to throb where she had hit the wooden doorway at her side. The wet street was again spread before her, the air still full of horrid bells. She sent one last rattled look inside the store and found the shopkeeper kneeling amongst his ruin. He held a can washed free of its label, a roll of undamaged toilet tissue in pink paper. His face was strange, as if it had collapsed into itself. He was making a low whistling sound through the gap in his teeth.

She took a step toward him without thinking, then

stopped. She hated herself for her first impulse, to comfort. The caretaker of others wasn't who she wanted to be—it was not her natural role—but it somehow had become who she was.

She watched herself as if from above as she moved back into the store, picking over the rubble. The shopkeeper stood as she neared. He smelled of wet denim and sweated-out alcohol and sour private skin. Up close, he looked at her face briefly, with a doggish expression, something both hungry and ashamed. Maybe he had a family, a wife who had worried when he hadn't returned in the night. Certainly, he, too, was the child of a mother who was either very old or dead.

He looked up at her, then he closed his eyes, as if she, this morning, was too much for him.

She reached out to touch him, but in the end, she couldn't. She took a step back and picked things up off the ground. A pen. A dustpan. A bath toy. She piled the items gently in his arms. And when he didn't move, she stooped to collect more: pens, cookies, a hand of bananas. One perfect orange, its pores even and clean.

FLOWER HUNTERS

―――

I t is Halloween; she'd almost forgotten.

At the corner, a man is putting sand and tea-light candles into white paper bags.

He will return later with a lighter, filling the dark neighborhood with a glowing grid for the trick-or-treaters.

She wonders if this is wise, whether it is not, in fact, incredibly dangerous to put flames near so many small uncoordinated people with polyester hems.

All day today and yesterday she has been reading the early naturalist William Bartram, who traveled through Florida in 1774; because of him, she forgot Halloween.

She's most definitely in love with that dead Quaker.

This is not to say that she is no longer in love with her husband; she is, but after sixteen years together, perhaps they have blurred at the edges of each other's vision.

She says to her dog, who is beside her at the window

watching the candle man, One day you'll wake up and realize your favorite person has turned into a person-shaped cloud.

The dog ignores her, because the dog is wise.

In any event, her husband will inevitably win, since Bartram takes the form of dead trees and dreams, and her husband takes the form of warm pragmatic flesh.

She picks up her cell—she wants to tell her best friend, Meg, about her sudden overwhelming love for the ghost of a Quaker naturalist—but then she remembers that Meg doesn't want to be her best friend anymore.

A week ago, Meg said very gently, I'm sorry, I just need to take a break.

Outside, in Florida, there's still the hot yellow wool of daylight.

In the kitchen, her sons are eating their dinner of bean tacos glumly.

They had wanted to be ninjas, but she had to concoct something quickly, and now their costumes are hanging up in the laundry room.

Earlier, she put her own long-sleeved white button-down backward on the younger boy, crossed the arms around and tied them in the back, added a contractor's mask she'd slitted and colored with a silver Sharpie, and because he was armless, she pinned a candy bucket to the waist.

Cannibal Lecture, he is calling himself, a little too on the nose.

For the older boy, she cut eyeholes in a white sheet for an old-style ghost, though it rankled, a white boy in a white sheet, Florida still the Deep South; she hopes that the effect is mitigated by the rosebuds along the hems.

She also forgot the kindergarten's Spooky Breakfast this morning; she'd failed to bring the boo-berry muffins, and her smaller son had sat in his regular clothes in his tiny red chair, looking hopefully at the door as mothers and fathers in their masks and wigs who kept not being her poured in.

She wasn't even thinking of him at that hour; she was thinking of William Bartram.

Her husband comes in from work, sees the costumes, raises an eyebrow, remains merciful.

The boys brighten as if on a dimmer switch, her husband turns on "Thriller" to get in the mood, and she watches them bop around, a twist in the heart.

It's not yet dusk, but the shadows have stretched.

Her husband puts on an old green Mohawk wig, the boys shimmy their costumes on again, and the three of them head out.

She is alone in the house with the dog and William Bartram and the bags of wan lollipops that were all that remained on the drugstore's shelves.

It's necessary to hand out candy; her first year in the house, she righteously gave out toothbrushes, and it wasn't an accident that a heavy oak branch smashed her window that night.

She can almost see three blocks away into the kitchen of Meg's house, where beautiful handmade costumes are being put on.

Meg loves this shit.

A week ago, when Meg broke up with her, they were eating ginger scones that Meg had made from scratch, and the bite in her mouth went so dry that she couldn't swallow for a long, long time.

She just nodded as Meg spoke kindly and firmly, and she felt each rip as her heart was torn into smaller and smaller pieces in Meg's capable hands.

Meg has enormous gray eyes and strong hips and shoulders, and hair like a glass of dark honey with sunshine in it.

Meg is the best person she knows, far better than herself or her husband, maybe even better than William Bartram.

Meg is the medical director of the abortion clinic in town, and all day she has to hold her patients' stories and their bodies, as well as the tragic lack of imagination from the chanting protesters on the sidewalk.

It would be too much for anyone, but it is not too much for Meg.

On the mantel in Meg's house, there are pictures of Meg with her children as babies, secured on her back, all three peering at the camera like koalas.

She, too, has often felt the urge to ride nestled cozily on Meg's back.

She would feel safe there, her cheek against her strongest friend.

But for the past week she has respected Meg's wish to take a break, and so she has not called Meg or stopped by her house for coffee or sent her children down the street to play with Meg's children until someone runs home screaming with a bruise or low blood sugar.

What is it about me that people need breaks from? she asks the dog, who looks as though she wants to say something but, out of innate gentleness, refrains.

A generous kind of dog, the labradoodle.

Well, William Bartram won't need a break from her.

The dead need nothing from us; the living take and take.

She brings William Bartram in his book costume out to the front porch, where it is cooler, and fetches the candy in a bowl and the dog and the wineglass so big it can hold a full bottle of ten-dollar Shiraz.

She settles herself under the bat lights she plugged in because she forgot to make jack-o'-lanterns and watches real bats swinging between the rooftops.

William Bartram seduced her with his drawings of horny turtles and dog-faced alligators, with his flights of ecstatic gratitude that lifted him toward God.

A week ago, after the ginger scones and suffocating with sadness, she took the afternoon off from work and drove to Micanopy to look at antiques, because she feels solace when she touches things that have survived generations of human hands.

She stood in the center of Micanopy hating her unsweet tea because it was encased in plastic foam that would disintegrate and float on the surface of the waters forever; but then she found the plaque about William Bartram, who had passed through Micanopy in 1774, when it was a Seminole trading post called Cuscowilla.

The chief there at the time was called the Cowkeeper.

When the Cowkeeper heard what Bartram was doing, traipsing about Florida collecting floral specimens and faunal observations, he nicknamed him Puc-Puggy.

This translates, roughly, to Flower Hunter, which—as bestowed upon Bartram by a warrior and hunter and proud owner of slaves he'd stripped from the many tribes he'd brutally subjugated—was probably no great compliment.

Still, what would bright-eyed Puc-Puggy have seen of Florida before the automobile, before the airplane, before the planned communities, before the swarms of Mouseketeers?

A damp, dense tangle.

An Eden of dangerous things.

A trio of witches comes up the walk, and not one says thank you when she drops her bad candy into their bags.

An infant dressed as a superhero, something like sweet potato crusted on his cheeks, looks on as his mother holds the pillowcase open for the treat and then clicks her tongue in disappointment.

But her street is a dark one and full of rentals, and the savvy trick-or-treaters mostly stay away.

It's just before twilight, and the sky is a brilliant orange.

She is inside the pumpkin.

In the absence of tiny ghouls, the lizards come out one last time, frilling their red necks, doing push-ups on the sidewalk.

Like Bartram, she was once a northerner dazzled by the frenzied flora and fauna here, but that was a decade ago, and things that once were alien life have become, simply, parts of her life.

She is no longer frightened of reptiles, she who is frightened of everything.

She is frightened of climate change, this summer the hottest on record, plants dying all around.

She is frightened of the small sinkhole that opened in the rain yesterday near the southeast corner of her house and may be the shy exploratory first steps of a much larger sinkhole.

She is frightened of her children, because now that they've arrived in the world she has to stay here for as long as she can but not longer than they do.

She is frightened because maybe she has already

become so cloudy to her husband that he has begun to look right through her; she's frightened of what he sees on the other side.

She is frightened that there aren't many people on the earth she can stand.

The truth is, Meg had said, back when she was still a best friend, you love humanity almost too much, but people always disappoint you.

Meg is someone who loves both humanity and people; William Bartram loved humanity and people and also nature.

He was a gifted and perceptive scientist who also believed in God, which seems a rather gymnastic form of philosophy.

She misses believing in God.

Here comes a prospector with a tiny pick; two scary teenage clowns in regular clothes; a courtly family, the parents crowned regents, the boy a knight in silver plastic, the girl a fluttery yellow princess.

What a relief that she has boys; this princess nonsense is a tragedy of multigenerational proportions.

Stop waiting for someone to save you, humanity can't even save itself! she says aloud to the masses of princesses seething in her brain; but it is her own black dog who blinks in agreement.

She reads by bat light and sees two William Bartrams as she does: the bright-eyed thirty-four-year-old explorer with the tan and sinewy muscles and sketchbook, besieged by alligators, comfortable supping alone with mosquitoes and with rich indigo planters alike, and also Bartram's older, paler self, in the quiet of his Pennsylvania garden, projecting his joy and his younger persona onto the page.

Both Bartrams, the feeling body and the remembering brain, show themselves in his descriptions of a bull gator: *Behold him rushing forth from the flags and reeds. His enormous body swells. His plaited tail brandished high, floats upon the lake. The waters like a cataract descend from his opening jaws. Clouds of smoke issue from his dilated nostrils. The earth trembles with his thunder.*

Usually, she's the one who trick-or-treats with the boys, with Meg and her three children, but this year Meg is out with Amara, a banker who is nice enough but who competes sneakily, through her children.

She can take Amara in small doses, the way she can take everyone except for her sons and her husband and Meg, the only four people on earth she could take in every dose imaginable to man.

Maybe, she thinks, Meg and Amara are talking about her.

They're not talking about me, she tells her dog.

Something has changed in the air; there's a lot of wind now, a sense of something lurking.

The spirits of the dead, she'd think, if she were superstitious.

The dark has thickened, and she hears music from the mansion down the road where every year the neighbors host an extravagant haunted house.

She is alone, and no trick-or-treaters have wandered by in an hour, the white sandbags of candlelight have burned out, and the renters have all turned off their lights, pretending not to be home.

She reads from Bartram's prologue, where he describes his hunter companion slaughtering a mother bear and then coming back mercilessly for the baby.

The continual cries of this afflicted child, bereft of its parent, affected me very sensibly, I was moved with compassion, and charging myself as if accessary to what now appeared to be a cruel murder, and endeavoured to prevail on the hunger to save its life, but to no effect! for by habit he had become insensible to compassion towards the brute creation, being now within a few yards of the harmless devoted victim, he fired, and laid it dead upon the body of the dam.

And now she is crying.

I'm not crying, she tells the dog, but the dog sighs deeply.

The dog needs to take a little break from her.

The dog stands and goes inside and crawls under the baby grand piano that she bought long ago from a lonely old lady, a piano that nobody plays.

A lonely old piano.

She always wanted to be the kind of person who could play the "Moonlight" Sonata.

She buries her failure in this, as she buries all her failures, in reading.

The wine is finished; she sucks a lollipop that only tastes red.

She reads for a long time until she hears what she thinks is her stomach growling, but it is, in fact, nearby thunder.

And just after the thunder comes the rain, and with the rain comes the memory of the baby sinkhole near the southeast corner of the house.

Her husband texts: the boys and he have taken shelter at the haunted house; there's tons of food, all their friends, so much fun, she should come!—but he knows her better than that, this would be the third circle of hell for her, she cannot abide parties, she could not abide any friends when she's lost the best one.

She can't even read Bartram anymore because the thought of the sinkhole is like a hole in the mouth where a tooth used to be.

She prods and prods the sinkhole in her mind.

The rain knocks at the metal roof, and she imagines it licking away at the limestone under her house, the way her children lick away at Everlasting Gobstoppers, which they are not allowed, but which she still somehow finds in sticky rainbow pools in their sock drawers.

The rain rains yet harder, and she puts on a yellow slicker and galoshes, and goes out with a flashlight.

Her face is being smacked by a giant hand, and another is smacking the crown of her head.

She puts a fist over her mouth to find the air to breathe and stands on the edge of the sinkhole, then crouches because the light is weak in the downpour.

No rain is collecting in the crater, which she thinks is extremely bad, because it must mean that the water is dripping through small cracks below, which means there's a place for the water to go, which means there is a cavity, and the cavity could be enormous, right there beneath her feet.

She becomes aware of a stream of water licking its way down the end of her hair and into the collar of her slicker, and then slipping coolly across the bare skin of her shoulder and then over her left breast and across her lower left rib cage and entering her navel and unfurling itself luxuriously over her right hip.

It feels remarkable, like a good cold blade across her skin.

It is erotic, she thinks, not the same thing as sexual.

Erotic is suckling her newborns, that animal smell and feel and warmth and tenderness.

Laying her head on her friend's shoulder and smelling the soap on her skin.

Letting the sun slide over her face without worrying about cancer or the ice caps melting.

She thinks of Bartram in the deep semitropical forest, far from his wife, aroused by the sight of an evocative blue flower that exists as a weed in her own garden, writing, in what is surely a double entendre or, if not, deeply

Freudian: *How fantastical looks the libertine Clitoria, mantling the shrubs, on the vistas skirting the groves!*

This, this is what she loves in Bartram so much!

The way he lets himself be full animal, a sensualist, the way he finds glory in the body's hungers and delights.

Florida, Bartram's ghost has been trying to tell her all along, is erotic.

For years now, she has been unable to see it all around her, the erotic.

The rain, impossibly, comes down harder, and even the flashlight is no help.

She is wet and alone and crouching in the dark over an unknowable hole, and now she locates the point of breakage.

Odd that it had taken so long.

Two weeks ago, she called Meg at eleven at night because she'd read an article about the coral reefs in the Gulf of Mexico being covered with a mysterious whitish slime that was killing them, and she knew enough to know that when a reef collapses, so do dependent populations, and when they go, the oceans go, and Meg had answered, as she always does, but she had just put her youngest back to bed, and she was weary after a long day of helping women, and she said, Hey, relax, you can't do anything about it, go drink the rest of the bottle of wine, take a bath, we can talk in the morning if you're still sad.

That was it, that last call.

Poor Meg.

She is exhausting to everyone.

She would take a break from herself, too, but she doesn't have that option.

For a minute, she lets herself imagine the larger sinkhole below the baby one opening very slowly and cupping her and the house and the dog and the piano all the way to the very black bottom of the limestone hollow and gently depositing them there so far down that nobody could get her out, they could only visit, her family's heads peering once in a while over the lip, tiny pale bits against the blue sky.

From down there, everyone would seem so happy.

She comes in from the rain.

The kitchen is too bright.

Surely, in the history of humanity, she is not the only one to feel like this.

Surely, in the history of herself, all of those versions atop previous versions, she has felt worse.

It was called the New World, but Puc-Puggy understood that there was nothing new about it, *as almost every step we take over those fertile heights, discovers remains and traces of ancient human habitations and cultivation.*

She takes off the wet boots, the wet jacket, the wet skirt, the wet shirt, and, shivering, picks up her phone to call her husband.

The dog is licking the rain off her knees with a warm and loving tongue.

If she says sinkhole, her husband will race home in the rain with her children and their goodies.

They will put the boys to bed and stand together at the lip of the sinkhole, and maybe she will become solid again.

And so, when he picks up, she will say, Babe, I think we have a problem, but she will say it in the warmest, softest voice she owns, having learned from a master the way to deliver bad news.

She lets her hunger for her husband's voice grow until she is almost incandescent with it.

As the phone rings and rings, she says to the dog, who is looking up at her, Well, nobody can say that I'm not trying.

ABOVE AND BELOW

━━━

She'd been kept awake all night by the palm berries clattering on the roof, and when she woke to the sun blazing through the window, she'd had enough. *Goodbye to all that!* she sang, moving the little she owned to the station wagon: her ex-boyfriend's guitar, the camping equipment they'd bought the first year of grad school (their single night on the Suwannee, they were petrified by the bellows of the bull gators), a crate of books. Goodbye to the hundreds of others she was leaving stacked against the wall. *Worthless,* the man had told her when she'd tried to sell them.

Goodbye to the mountain of debt she was slithering out from underneath. Goodbye to the hunter-orange eviction notice. Goodbye to longing. She would be empty now, having chosen to lose.

The apartment was a shell, scoured to enamel. She breathed fully when she stepped out onto the porch.

There was a brief swim of vertigo only when she shooed the cat out the door. Oh, you'll be all right, she said, and reached for the silky fur between his ears, but as quick as a blink, he struck at her. When she looked up from the four jagged lines slowly beading with blood on the back of her hand, he had leapt away. Then he, too, was gone.

She drove past the brick university, where the first-years were already unloading their sedans, their parents hugging their own shoulders for comfort. Goodbye, she said aloud to the tune of the tires humming on the road.

After a summer with the power shut off, a summer of reading by the open window in her sweat-soaked under-wear, the car's air conditioner felt frigid. She opened the window and smelled the queer dank musk of deep-country Florida. Out here, people decorated their yards with big rocks and believed they could talk to God. Here, "Derrida" was only French for rear end.

She thrust her fist out the window and released it slowly. She could almost see her hopes peeling from her palm and skipping down the road in her wake: the books with her name on them; the sabbatical in Florence; the gleaming modern house at the edge of the woods. Gone.

When she looked at her hand again, it was puffy and hot and oozing. She put it to her mouth. When she stopped at last at the edge of a little oceanside town and gazed over the dune grass at the sea, her tongue was coppery with the taste of blood.

Someone had left a cooler on the beach, and it still held a bag of apples, a half-eaten sandwich, two Cokes. She sat, watching the dusk turn mustard and watermelon, and ate everything. Seabirds clustered on the wet sand, then winged apart into the air. When it grew too dark for her to see, she took the cooler back to the car and walked up to A1A to a pay phone.

She was poised to hang up if her stepfather answered, but it was her mother, vague and slow, saying Hello? Hello?

She couldn't speak. She imagined her mother in her nightgown in the kitchen, a sunset, the neighbor kids playing outside.

Hello? her mother said again, and she managed, Hello, Mom.

Honey, her mother said. What a treat to hear from you.

Mom, she said. I just wanted to let you know that I moved. I don't have a new number yet, though.

She waited, feeling the sunburn begin to prickle in her cheeks, but her mother said only, Is that so? absently. Ever since she'd been remarried, she'd had chronic idiopathic pain, treated, also chronically, with painkillers. She hadn't remembered her daughter's birthday for three years; she'd sent empty care packages more than once. One hot July day, when the girl had stared at her sickening bank balance at the ATM, she'd considered calling for help. But she'd known, somehow, that the envelope would also arrive empty.

Over the line, there was the sound of an engine drawing close, and her mother said, Oh! Your dad's home. They both listened to the slam of the door and the heavy boots on the steps, and she thought but didn't say, That man is not my dad.

Instead she said, Mom, I just want you to not worry if you don't hear from me for a while. Okay? I'm all right, I promise.

All right, honey, her mother said, her voice already softer, anticipating her husband's arrival. Don't do anything I wouldn't do.

As the girl walked back on the road, headlights spinning by in the dark, she said aloud, I'm doing exactly what you would do, and laughed, but it wasn't very funny after all.

During the day, she lay in the sun for hours until she was so thirsty she had to fill her camping water bottle at the fish-washing hose again and again. In the rearview mirror, she watched her skin toast and her hair shift from honey to lemon. Her clothes flapped on her. She thought of the thousands of dollars she'd spent on highlights over the years: all that anguish, all those diets, when all she needed to be pretty was laziness and some mild starvation!

She ate cans of tuna and sleeves of crackers and drank an occasional coffee from the beach café for pep. Her money dwindled alarmingly. The scar on her hand turned a lovely silver in the sun, and she sometimes stroked it absently, signifier in lieu of signified, the scratch for the lost life.

At night, she lay in the back of the station wagon and read *Middlemarch* with a penlight until she fell asleep.

When she smelled too strong for salt water to rinse the stink away, she walked into the gym of a fancy beachside condo complex in her running clothes. She waited for someone to yell at her, but nobody was watching. The bathroom was empty, and the vanities held baskets with lotions, tiny soaps, disposable razors. She stood in the shower and let her summer of loneliness wash away. Even before her boyfriend left her for a first-year master's student, she'd withdrawn into herself. Her funding hadn't been renewed, and she'd had only her TA stipend, which was barely enough for her half of the rent, let alone groceries. There was no going out, even if she could have swallowed her shame to look her funded friends in the eye. The boyfriend had taken everything with him: their Sunday brunches, the etiquette book he had unsubtly given her one Christmas, the alarm clock that woke them ten minutes before six every day. He had been a stickler for the proper way to do things—hospital corners, weight lifting, taking notes—and he'd stolen her routine from her when he left. Worst of all, he'd taken his parents, who had welcomed her for four years of holidays in their generous stone house in Pennsylvania. For weeks, she had expected the mother, a soft-haired, hugging woman, to call her, but there was no call.

The door opened and voices flooded the bathroom, some aerobics class letting out. She turned to wash her face in the spray, suddenly shy. When she opened her eyes, the showers were full of naked middle-aged women laughing and soaping themselves. They wore diamond bands and their teeth shone and their bellies and thighs were larded by their easy lives.

She woke to a hard rapping next to her ear and struggled up through sleep into darkness. She turned on her penlight to see a groin in stretched black fabric and a shining leather belt hung with a gun in a holster and an enormous flashlight.

Cop, she thought. Penis of death, penis of light.

Open up, the policeman said, and she said, Yes, sir, and slid over the backseat and rolled down the window.

What are you smiling at? he said.

Nothing, sir, she said, and turned off her penlight.

You been here a week, he said. I been watching you.

Yes, sir, she said.

It's illegal, he said. Now, I get a kid once in a while doesn't want to pay for a motel, okay. I get some old hippies in their vans. But you're a young girl. Hate to see you get hurt. There are bad guys everywhere, you know?

I know, she said. I keep my doors locked.

He snorted. Yeah, well, he said. Then he paused. You run away from your man? That the story? There's a safe house for ladies up in town. I can get you in.

No, she said. There's no story. I guess I'm on vacation from my life.

Well, he said, and the looseness in his voice was gone. Get on out of here. Don't let me see you back, or I'll take you in for vagrancy.

S he spent a few days on a different beach where people drove their trucks onto the sand and pumped out music until their batteries ran down. She dug again into the wagon's seats to find change for a candy bar but failed, then she walked the miles into town to consider what she should do, her legs shaking by the time she arrived.

The buildings on the town square looked like old Florida—the tall porches with fans, the tin roofs—but everything was made of a dense plastic in shades of beige. There was a fountain in the center: a squat frog spitting up water and change scattered on the blue tiles under the water. She sat on the edge of the fountain and watched the shoppers in the boutiques and the people eating ice cream cones.

At one corner of the square stood a small brick church flanked by blooming crape myrtles. She didn't notice the people gathering in front until they began to emerge with hands full of styrofoam clamshells and juice packs. Some were stringy, greasy, the familiar life-beaten people who lived half visibly at the edge of the university town she'd come from. But there were also construction workers in hard hats, mothers hurrying away with kids in their wakes.

She wanted to stand. To be in the line, to get the food. Her body, though, wouldn't move. In the twilight, a family passed, and she thought how she had once been this blonde toddler on her tricycle, singing to herself while her parents walked behind her. How sudden the disturbance had been! Her father dead when she was ten, the struggle with money through high school, her mother marrying in exhaustion only to fold herself entirely away. The one safe place the girl had had left was school. But she'd been too careful in the end, unable to take the necessary scholarly risks, and they had withdrawn even that from her.

She sat like a second frog on the edge of the fountain, hunched over her hunger, until the clock clicked to an impossibly late hour and she was alone. She rolled up her jeans and stepped into the water. She felt along the bottom with her feet until she came upon a coin, and dipped her arm up to her shoulder, but almost all the change was glued to the tile. By the time she had gone entirely around, she had gathered only a small handful. When she peered at the coins in the dim light from the streetlamp, she found they were mostly pennies. Still, she went around again. She saw herself from a great distance, a woman stooping in knee-deep water for someone else's wishes.

Most days, she found food—bread and bruised fruit—
heaped, clean, in a dumpster behind a specialty grocer.
She hid the station wagon at the far end of a supermarket
parking lot, next to a retention pond and shielded by the
low branches of a camphor tree. The smell entered her
dreams at night, and she'd wake to a slow green sway of
branches, as if underwater. There was a Baudelaire poem
this reminded her of, but it had been erased from her
memory. She wondered what else was gone, the Goethe,
the Shakespeare, the Montale. The sun was bleaching it
all to dust; her hunger was eating it up. It was a cleansing,
she decided. If pretty words couldn't save her, then losing
them, too, was all for the best.

She was baking on the beach when a leaf slid up over
her stomach. She caught idly at it and found that it
wasn't a leaf at all but a five-dollar bill.

That night, she went into the poolside showers of an
apartment complex and washed herself carefully. When
she caught sight of herself naked in the mirror, she could
see the ribs of her upper chest and the pulse in the curve
of her hip bone. But she blow-dried her hair and put it
into a ponytail and applied makeup that she'd bought a
few years ago. She no longer looked like herself: diligent,
plump, prim. She looked like a surfer girl or a sorority
sister, one of those quivering dewy creatures she had always silently disliked.

She walked three miles to a beach bar, listening to the ocean break itself again and again. The place was full when she came up through the back door, the huge televisions blaring a football game. Once, she would have been invested in the game, if only because it was the lingua franca of the southern town, the way to put a freshman comp class at ease, to converse with a dean's vapid wife. But now it seemed silly to her, young men grinding into one another, war games muted with padding.

She ordered the dollar-special beer and gave the bartender another dollar for a tip. His fingers brushed hers when he handed her the change, and she was startled at the warmth of his skin. She peeled the label of her beer and took deep breaths.

Someone climbed onto the stool beside hers, and she looked at him when he ordered two gin and tonics. He was a sweet-looking sandy boy with large red ears, the kind of student who always got a B- in her classes, mostly on effort alone. He slid one of the drinks toward her shyly, and when he began to speak, he didn't stop. He was a junior up north but had had to take a semester off and was working in his mother's real estate office for now, which really pissed off the old agents there, because there were few enough commissions right now, real estate going to shit in this shitty, shitty time. And on and on. After three drinks, she was drunker than she'd ever let herself be. She wondered, as he spoke, what had happened to make him take a semester off. Drugs? A hazing scandal?

Bad grades? When they stopped on the walk to his place and he pressed her shoulders against the cold metal of a streetlight and kissed her with touching earnestness, she felt the soft hair at the base of his neck and thought he'd probably had a nervous breakdown. He kissed like a boy prone to anxiety attacks.

But she liked him, and his apartment was clean and pretty: she could sense the hand of an overbearing mother in its furnishings. Before he touched her, he looked at her naked body for a long time, blinking. She saw herself, then, as he did: the clean white of her bikini pressed into her skin, the eroticism of the contrast. In gratitude, she came toward him.

But afterward, the softness of the bed was overwhelming. As the boy slept, she went to the kitchen and opened the refrigerator. It was so full, the abundance stilled her. She ate a slice of cold pizza standing in the glow, opened a jar of pickles and ate three, ripped a hunk of cheddar from the block with her fingers and gobbled it down. She didn't see the boy standing in the doorway until she reached for the orange juice. Then she noticed the pale gleam of his T-shirt, and she closed her eyes, unable to look at him.

She could hear him walking toward her and steeled herself for recrimination. But he touched the small of her back and said a soft Oh, honey; and this was infinitely worse.

A hurricane developed over the Caribbean, but only its edges lashed the shore. Still, during the scream and blow, the camphor rattled its branches against the top of the car, and the wagon shook so hard she was afraid the metal would twist and the glass would break. The retention pond overflowed and water licked up to the hubcaps. She lay as quietly as she could and listened and watched: she was a thin shell of glass and steel from the raw nerve at the center of herself. She felt the storm come closer, charging near; she waited with a painful breathless patience. But before it arrived, she fell asleep.

She called her mother on Thanksgiving, but her stepfather answered and said her mother was in bed again, under the weather. Not that she cared. They'd given up on her coming home, but couldn't she call her damn mother once a month?

She held the receiver up to the highway and let him speak himself out, and in a pause, she said to tell her mother that she loved her and would call again soon. She sat for a while on a dune, shivering in the cold wind. The ocean was blank and inexpressive, withholding sympathy. At last, she was numbed enough that she could walk to the town and stand in the long line outside the church.

Today they were serving people in seatings, and the line moved very slowly.

Most of the people at the table looked normal. Across from her was a family, the mother with a chic black haircut and tattoos across her collarbone, the father with an artful mullet, the two little girls with barrettes in their bangs. Next to her was an enormous woman whose flesh pressed up to hers, firm and warm. Nobody spoke. There was a soup course—homemade minestrone with good bread— then the turkey course with canned everything: cranberries, mashed potatoes, stuffing, gravy, beans. And last, there were homemade pecan and pumpkin pies with coffee.

When the woman serving their table bent over to clear the pie plates, the large lady grasped her gloved hand. They all looked up to see the serving woman's startled face under her shower cap. Thank you, the large lady said, that was goooood, and the little girls laughed. The girl expected awkwardness, a hurrying away, but the serving woman briefly laid her cheek atop the lady's head and gave her a squeeze, and both women closed their eyes and leaned closer in.

I t had been a rare warm day, and she'd built wind walls out of sand and soaked the last of the season's sunshine into her skin. Now she dropped her towel and book and water, and stared in wonder at the station wagon. All the doors were open, her things spilling out. Her car had been gutted; her things were entrails. The hood was open, the engine gone. The tires were gone, the hubcaps gone, the front seats gone. Inside, a strong stench of urine: someone had pissed in the glove box. The guitar was gone, the camping stove, the tent, her childhood stuffed turtle, her winter jacket. *Middlemarch*, of all fucking things, gone. Her backpack had a long slit in it.

She gathered up what she could—the sleeping bag, *Paradise Lost*, some clothes, a tarp. She found some dental floss and a needle, and sewed up the backpack. Then she took the registration from the glove box and ripped it up—wet, it tore easily—and tossed the license plate into the retention pond, where it floated on the duckweed for a moment before it sank.

How light she thought she had been before. How truly light she was now.

She should be leaving anyway—it was too cold now, with the wind off the ocean. There were Santas in the store windows, in piles of fake snow.

Out on A1A, the cars screamed by her and threw exhaust in her face. She stuck out her thumb, and a tan sedan rolled to a stop. The driver was pale and nervous, and somewhere inside her alarm bells began to ring, but she found she didn't care to listen. He said he was going back to the university town, and she thought of her ex, her friends, her fall from safety. She found she didn't care about those things, either.

She could feel the ocean pulling at her back but didn't turn to say goodbye. It had failed to do what she had longed for it to do; it had been indifferent, after all. Over the inland waterway, with its tiny islands and corrugated bridge, into the palmetto scrub. Somewhere along a stretch of road bordered by pines in strict formation, the man put a hand on her knee and squinted toward the empty asphalt ahead. She gently removed his hand, and he didn't try again. He turned on the radio, and they listened to sticky love ballads. In town, he dropped her at the downtown plaza and squealed away, to the loud derision of two old men at the bus stop. They grinned at her and both blew pink bubbles with their gum and one by one let them pop.

Just before the public library closed for the night, she rode the elevator to the top floor and went into the grand stained-glass conference room set like a crown at the top of the building. She'd discovered an unlocked closet behind a leaning blackboard, barely long enough to hold her body in its sleeping bag. In the dark of the closet, she ate what she found during the day and listened to the library empty out. It was orange season, and she plucked satsumas for breakfast and spat the pips into the road.

She neglected to call her mother for Christmas or New Year's. When she tried to read during the day, the words lost their meaning and floated loosely in her eyes.

———

She didn't make it to the library in time one evening and spent the night shivering in her light jean jacket. She was walking by a club that had just closed when a cluster of undergraduates in strapless dresses tottered by, fingering their cell phones. She recognized one of them, a girl from her comp-lit class last year. She'd been a frightened, silent thing who'd earned her C-. No matter how hard she was drilled, "its" and "it's" had eluded the girl. Tonight, if she and the girl came face-to-face, the girl would look through her former instructor, not seeing her in this worn, dirty woman; and she, whose words had once lashed, would have nothing to say.

Its, it's, she said aloud now. Who cares?

A man stacking the chairs in front of the patio area heard her and laughed. Twits, he agreed.

She leaned against the railing and watched him work. He was a skinny, short brown man and exceptionally fast: he'd already rolled up the rubber mats and was hosing down the bricks when she realized he was still talking to her. I'm telling you, he was saying, sillier and sillier each damn day, filling up those heads with tweeters and scooters and facebooks and starbooks and shit. He looked up at her and grinned. His front four teeth were gone, and it gave him the mischievous air of a six-year-old. Name's Eugene, but everyone calls me Eugene-Euclean. I clean, right? I got three of these clubs to set right before morning, so's I can't stop to chat.

Okay, she said, and took a step, but he meant that he couldn't stop; he could still chat. This land, he told her, was full of living twits and unsettled spirits, both. The spirits were loud and unhappy, and filled the place with evil. All them dead Spanish missionaries and snake-bit Seminoles and starved-to-death Crackers and shit. He, Eugene-Euclean, came down from Atlanta near on four years back and got infected with the spirits and they were inside him and he couldn't find his way to leave.

By now, they were inside the booze-stinking club, and Eugene had poured her a glass of cranberry juice. He began to mop the floor with a bleach solution so strong it made her eyes water. He looked up at her and stopped, struck by a thought. I like you, he said. You keep your words in tight.

Thanks, Eugene, she said.

I could use some help, he said. Three clubs is hard to clean alone by morning-time come. You could do bathrooms, stuff like that. You got you a job?

No, she said.

He looked at her shrewdly and said, Fifty bucks Thursday, Friday, Saturday nights, twenty bucks other nights. Monday off.

She blinked at the empty bucket he thrust into her hands. Partner, he said.

There was a sensation in cleaning that she used to get in her other lifetime when the books she was reading were so compelling they carried her through the hours. Words were space carved out of life, warm and safe. Polishing windows to perfect clarity, scrubbing porcelain, working caustic chemicals into the tiles until they gleamed like teeth; all this detached her mind from herself. She grew hard muscles in her skinny arms.

In the mornings, she would walk into the cold and feel herself wrung out. Eugene-Euclean sometimes bought her breakfast, and they'd sit, stinking of chemicals, in their booth, surrounded by the smells of warm grease and hot coffee. She wanted to laugh with him, to tell him of the horror of her mother's house when she was little, the cockroaches and the dirt-crusted linoleum, how strange it was that she was cleaning now; but Eugene spoke so much she had no need to say anything. He'd tell her about this talking dog when he was a kid, or he'd describe his moments of illumination, when the world slowed and the Devil spoke in his ear until he was chased away by the brightness that grew inside Eugene and bathed the world in light.

She took a room by the week in a squat concrete motel sticking out over the highway. It was called Affordable— Best Price—Comfortable, but she had to borrow some chemicals and rags from Eugene to make the bathroom usable. She liked the sound of the trucks rumbling past and the steady rhythms of her neighbors' voices and the boys who hung out at the roasted-chicken place next door, with their swooping boasts and hoots of derision.

One morning, she was walking home to the motel when she saw a familiar bicycle at the coffee shop where she used to grade papers. She looked in the window, hiding her face with her baseball cap. Two of her former friends sat at a table, both frowning into their laptops. How fat they looked, how *pink*. They were nursing their plain black coffees, and she remembered, with a surge of ugliness, how they all used to complain that they were too poor for lattes. How rich they had been. It was a kind of wealth you don't know you have until you stand shivering outside in the morning, watching what you used to be. One of her friends, the man, sensing eyes upon him, slowly looked up. A knot pulled tight in her gut, but when he looked past her to a sleek young woman gliding by on a bicycle, the knot frayed and broke apart.

One Saturday in March, at their last club, she looked up to see Eugene-Euclean swaying on his feet. He was staring at the air ducts above with a taut look of ecstasy on his face. She couldn't get to him before he fell over. His body was rigid, his jaw grinding. She considered an ambulance, then dismissed it, because he had no money for medical care: he was saving for a bridge for his missing teeth. He always came out of it, he had told her. The Devil couldn't match the light in him. All she had to do was wait.

She went back to cleaning. When she was finished, she polished all the glasses and wiped the fur of dust from the bottles on the top shelves. She squeegeed the windows. When people in work clothes began passing by outside, it was time. When she came near Eugene-Euclean, however, she smelled a terrible odor and found that he had voided his bowels. She heaved him into a chair and dragged him to the bathroom and cleaned him as well as she could. She threw his pants and underwear and socks and shoes into the dumpster and fashioned a kind of loincloth from her sweatshirt. His van was parked in the lot, and she wrestled him up into the back and laid him out on a bundle of clean rags.

She didn't know where he lived or if he had loved ones. She hadn't asked anything about him, had only listened to what he'd chosen to tell. She left a note on his chest and locked the van, and when she returned in the afternoon to check on him, the van was gone, and he was gone, and though she waited for him at the clubs every night for the next week, none of the hungry, idle people in the plaza or the nightclub managers or the people at the shelter knew or would tell her where he was.

———————

A cold wind blew in one April night and killed the most fragile plants. Across town, there were skeletons of ferns and banana plants and camellias. In the morning, the small, frowning Thai woman who owned Affordable—Best Price—Comfortable knocked on the door and waited in the doorway, silent and cross-armed, until the girl had packed up, put on her shoes and jacket, and left the room.

At noon, she followed the slow-moving parade of the indigent to the plaza and received a sandwich in plastic and a can of juice. At six, she followed them to the Methodist church and was served milk with a sour taste she remembered from kindergarten and a baked potato with chili.

Afterward, she followed a group past the homeless shelter, which was always full by one minute past five, when it opened for the night. They passed the old town depot, went through a park scarred with chain-link fences and heaps of dirt. They came out onto the bike path where she and her ex, once upon a time, had taken long, leisurely rides to see the alligators glistening on the banks of the sinkhole pools. It was dark in the woods, thick with Spanish moss and vines that looked from the corners of her eyes like snakes. She felt a new uprising in her, a sharp fear, and tried to swallow it. The people ahead of her disappeared off the bike path and into the trees.

She could smell it before she saw it: the tang of urine

and shit and woodsmoke and spilled beer and something starchy boiling. She heard the voices and came out into a clearing. In the dark, tents hulked beyond where she could see them, and there were fires here and there.

A man shouted, You looking for me, sweetheart? and there were laughs and she could see a dark shape detaching from the closest fire and gliding toward her.

She heard a woman's voice behind her saying warmly, There you are! and she felt herself being pushed past the man who approached, then past seven or eight campfires.

They stopped. Hang on, the woman said, and she bent down and held a lighter to a newspaper, then the newspaper to a bit of kindling. The fire revealed a heavy woman with a bready face and hair in a pink shade of red. I got the water, kids, she said. You can come out. There was the sound of a zipper, and four little bodies crept from a tent. They were indistinguishable from one another at first, four skinny things with long blondish hair.

The woman looked up and said, Not smart, coming here alone.

I had nowhere to go, she said, and her voice sounded ugly in her ears.

No family? the woman said. Clean-looking girl like you?

No, she said.

Got food? the woman asked, and she nodded as she pulled from her pack the last of her supplies: a loaf of white bread, a jar of peanut butter, a pack of cheese, a few tins of sardines, three cheap dry packs of ramen.

Peanut butter! one of the kids said, snatching it up, and the woman smiled at her for the first time. Share your food, you can share our tent, she said.

Thank you, she said. When they sat to eat, one of the little girls came close to her and put a hand on the sole of her foot. When she was little, she'd had the same hunger for touch. She could smell woodsmoke in the girl's blond hair, something clovelike in her skin.

The big woman was named Jane, and they nursed cups of weak cocoa after the children went to sleep. Jane told her about the husband who had run off, the house she and the kids lost, the jobs she'd been fired from because of her temper. She sighed. Same old story, she said.

She could hear the campsite settling, could smell marijuana over the thick stink of the place; a man was shouting, then his voice suddenly cut off. The house was real nice, Jane said ruefully. Pool and all. My husband always said there's no such thing as a Florida childhood without a pool. She snorted, and made a gesture toward the children. Now we're camping.

How long have you been here? the girl asked.

But this was the wrong thing to say, and Jane frowned at her and said, It's temporary, and stood to clean her cup. We'll get back to where we were.

Still, when she went to brush her teeth, she noticed Jane watching. Toothpaste, she said. Kids've been out for a while. You think tomorrow you can let us borrow some? And she said sure, and Jane smiled again, and by the time the two women went into the tent and curled on either side of the four sprawling children, they were friends again.

In the bright light of the morning, the campsite was steaming with fog: it looked almost innocuous, dreamy. She started up the fire and found the drinking water and began to boil oatmeal for the kids. They came out, one by one. The oldest couldn't have been more than five, none of them school age. In other tents, other women's voices rose, other children responded. A small boy ran over, said a shy Hey to Jane's children, and fled back to his mother.

She understood now that this was the family part of the tent city, that the safety here was safety in numbers, of rules and unspoken militancy against the threat just feet beyond.

Jane poked her head out, smiled, and emerged in a fast-food uniform.

You watch the kids today? she said. The girl who usually watches them got housing a few days ago, and I better not drop them at the library again.

I can read, the oldest girl said. I can, too, the second-oldest said. Sort of, the first said, but kindly.

She looked at the children, a sinking in her stomach. Oh, she said.

Jane's face was cold again. Listen, she said. Either I work or we never get out of here. Either they stay with you or I drop them off at the library and risk Family Services catching wind and lose them. We got no choice.

Okay, she said. Of course I'll watch them. And Jane said thanks but looked at her sourly as she untangled the little girls' hair with a wet comb.

Nights, Jane came back stinking of grease, with bags of burgers and fries that had sat for too long to sell. She soaked her feet in warm water, groaning, and, when the kids were asleep, talked bitterly of her boss. Stupid young lech, she said. Felt up my boobies in the supply room.

The girl nodded, listening, offering little. But Jane seemed to take solace in her quiet presence, treating her like a slow cousin, pitiful but useful.

The kids and she were coming out of the library one afternoon when they saw Jane across the street on a bench.

Uh-oh, the oldest girl said. The youngest buried her head in her brother's back.

Stay here, she said, and sat the children on a wall in front of the library.

Fired, Jane said, without raising her head. I got a temper. I *told* you that.

It's all right, she said, though the ground seemed to buckle under her feet. You'll get another job.

Jane lifted her head and spat, No, it isn't all right. It's so not fucking all right. I put down all our money on a place the other day and was waiting for my pay on Friday to put down the rest.

Jane sighed and passed a hand over her face and said, Go back to the tent. I'll be in when I'm in.

For supper, she and the kids had tomato soup and cheese sandwiches. She told the children stories filched from the *Arabian Nights*, and they fell asleep waiting for their mother. She sat by the fire until she ran out of wood and the bodies drifting by in the darkness grew menacing. Then she zipped herself inside the tent, warmed by the breath of the children.

In the morning, Jane's side of the tent was still empty. She took the children to the graveyard halfway between the tent city and the town. It was their favorite place: calm, neat, and pretty, with great old oaks and rows of plastic flowers that they gathered in their arms and redistributed to the loneliest-looking stones.

At the end of the day, she brought the children to the police department and gave them each a cup of oversweetened tea and a powdered doughnut that she found on a table in the waiting area.

When she asked about Jane, the policewoman barely looked up from her computer. She sucked her lip and typed in Jane's name and said, Um-hum. Arrested yesterday at about seven. Prostitution.

No, the girl said. The children were out of earshot. She said, That can't be right.

The policewoman flicked her eyes over her, and the girl could see herself as the woman did—dirty, stringy, smelly, browned to leather, clearly homeless. The policewoman's mouth settled into its wrinkles. Well, it is, she said, and went back to what she was doing.

The girl summoned the ghost of the almost-professor she'd been and said, enunciating sharply, Officer, please listen to me. I need to have you contact Family Services. These are Jane's children and I find that I cannot, unfortunately, care for them at this time.

She sat with the children until a tired-looking woman in a black suit hurried in, stopping to talk with the officer at the desk. When the Family Services woman said a bright Hello, the kids looked up from the magazine they'd been studying and watched warily as the woman hoisted her trousers to crouch before them.

The girl stood, her knees wobbly, and backed toward the door.

The day was too bright. Her head rang. She had eaten nothing since the morning. She went back to the tent and slept until dawn. Just before the tent city began to stir, she gathered her things and walked to town, leaving Jane's tent still up, the children's belongings tidied into piles and her own sleeping bag in the center in craven apology.

She thought of her mother, what it must be like for her to have a vanished daughter. The police must have found the abandoned station wagon and traced it; someone must have called. Her mother would think of murder or abduction, would wonder what she had done to make her daughter so ungrateful. Maybe, the girl thought with a pulse of spite, fear had finally awakened her mother. Maybe she was scouring the state for her, even now.

She slept for two days under her tarp in her former neighbor's bamboo thicket. The nights were warmer in May, but she still shivered. Once, she woke to find the bright green eyes of a cat staring at her and called out her old pet's name, but the animal ran off.

She walked all the way to the university, remembering that it was graduation weekend, which meant that many of the students were moving out. Perhaps she could get some food or another sleeping bag, she thought. In college, she had watched boys open a fifth-floor fraternity window and dump their perfectly good computers to the ground. She herself had emptied her mini fridge of its still-fresh yogurts and apples and frozen pizzas, and tossed them into the garbage. She felt ratlike on campus, scuttling from shadow to shadow. If anyone she knew saw her. If anyone smelled her. There was a tent in one quad, and she could just perceive in the dawn that a buffet was being set up. She waited until the caterers went behind their van for a break, and swiftly filled up a plate with hot eggs and potatoes and sausage. She looked up to see one of the caterers staring at her, a crate of glasses in his hands. She smiled at him, and he, grimly, waved her off.

Outside the senior dorms, she noticed a great metal truck into which people were heaving mattresses, coffee makers, chairs. She saw an office chair levitate above the lip of a dumpster, but the boy who was supposed to catch it had already seized a crate of electrical wires and turned away. The arms holding it began to shake. Without thinking, she stepped forward and grasped the chair above her head. The man who was passing it peeked out at her, smiling. He had black hair tied back in a ponytail and crow's-feet pressed into the skin beside his eyes. You helping? he said.

She was surprised into saying, Sure.

He winked and passed over a rolled-up rug.

She carried boxes of books, a headboard, a coffee table. The truck suddenly started up and someone muttered, Come on. She ran as the others began to run and leapt with them into the truck. A security car pulled up just as the doors clanged shut and the truck moved off. It was dark, the engine roaring, so crowded she felt as if she were suffocating. But someone touched her arm, lightly traced it to her hand, and put something paper-covered into her palm. It was a candy bar.

At last, the truck stopped and the engine shut off. There was a clicking, and the doors opened to impossible brightness. They were at the edge of a long rolling expanse of grass. She heaved her backpack down and jumped out onto the sandy ground.

A girl with a smudged face and long braid turned to her and said, It's breakfast time.

She trailed the other girl up the dirt drive to a sprawling ramshackle building. What is this? she said, and the other girl laughed. It's the Prairie House, she said. It's a squat. Do you normally just follow people without knowing where you're going?

Recently, yes, she said. The girl looked carefully at her, then said, Whoa. You don't look so good, sweetie, and led her to a bed that she sank into even though the sheets smelled strongly of someone else and she couldn't find the energy to take off her boots.

She slept through the day, the night, the next day, and woke light-headed with hunger. She crept down to the kitchen, passing bodies sprawled on cots and mattresses. The refrigerator was nauseating, overstuffed and sending off a garlicky rotten odor, but she found a pot of stew that was still warm shoved in among wrinkled apples.

The moon had risen over the prairie and shot the hummocks with shadow. A small creature was moving at the edge of the lawn, and in the house, she could hear the others sleeping, their movements and breath. She was alert, as she hadn't been in years. She turned on the light over the stove and looked at it in horror: it was caked with old meals, stinking of grease. She would begin now, she thought, and found a cleaner under the sink, a mismatched pair of rubber gloves, some steel wool. She began inch by inch and worked as quietly as she could. She avoided the windows, sensing that if she looked out, she would see Eugene's hungry spirits massing up from the prairie, the Crackers with their whips, the malarial conquistadores on their little ponies. Or Jane's children, their faces pressed to the glass.

By morning, the stove shone, the refrigerator was clean and the rotten food tossed, the dishes in the sink scoured and the sink again its natural stainless-steel color. She had reordered the cabinets, cleaning them of mouse droppings and dead cockroaches.

Her body felt vague with fatigue, but the clarity in her head remained. When she turned around, the man from the dumpster was sitting at the table watching her. Wowzers, he said. Can't remember the last time somebody made this kitchen so shiny.

I still have a lot to do, she said, and he said, Sit down a minute and talk.

He told her the rules: No fighting, no drugs, sleep where you find a place. People were in and out all the time and nobody knew everyone, so if she had valuables, she'd need to keep them close.

I have nothing, she said, and he said, All the better. Everyone pulls their weight, doing things around the house or in the barn, where they had a business reselling discarded items on the Internet, which paid for the water and electric and some of the food they didn't just salvage. They tried to live without money as much as possible and did pretty well.

He stopped and grinned at her.

That's it? she said. Even in the tent city there had been more implicit rules.

Yup, he said. It's heaven.

She thought for a minute and said, Or hell.

Same difference, he said, and poured her a coffee.

The party had grown organically, as things did in the Prairie House. Now there were skinny-dippers, splashes of surprising white in the sinkhole, and a keg circled by Christmas lights strung up on an oak tree. She turned from the bonfire where she was standing, the silhouettes of dancing bodies still in her eyes.

Beyond the party, the prairie unscrolled, calm and impassive, meeting the sky with an equal darkness. She found herself moving into it, each step a relief from the drunken voices, the flaming moths of paper spun from the fire, the sear of the flames. Past the first hummock of trees, the darkness took on a light of its own, and she began to distinguish the texture of the ground. She moved calmly over the pits of sand, palmettos biting at her calves, strange sudden seeps of marsh. Small things rustled away from her footsteps, and she felt fondly toward them, for their smallness and their fear.

After ten minutes, human noise had scaled to nothing, and insect noise took on urgency. Her body was slick with sweat. When she stopped, she felt the first itch. She kept herself still and was so quiet for so long that the prairie began its furtive movements again. The world that, from the comfort of the fire, had seemed a cool wiped slate was unexpectedly teeming.

She could smell the rot of a drainage ditch some well-meaning fools had dug through the prairie during the Depression. The land had taken the imprint of their hands and made it its own. She thought of the snakes sleeping coiled in their burrows and the alligators surfacing to scent her in the darkness, their shimmy onto the land, their stealthy bellying; how she was only one living lost thing among so many others, not special for being human. Something crawled across her throat.

She was frozen. The sweat cooled on her body and

made her shiver. There was no relief in the sky vaguely filmed with stars, a web vaster than she could imagine. There was nobody around, nobody to deliver her back to the solace of people.

The night on the prairie returned to her during the long and terrible birth of her daughter, years later, after her mother's funeral on a hill white with sleet. A shot in the spine took the pain away, and she floated above herself, safe in the beeping of the machines.

But something went wrong very suddenly. The nurses' faces pressed in; the world shifted to frenzy. She was wheeled into a cold room. It was almost Christmas and a poinsettia hunched in the corner, making her think of the black dirt in the pot, all the life there. Her body shook so hard it rattled the aluminum slab she was lying on. There was an unbearable pressure inside her as the doctor pushed the knife in. Then the old panic returned, the darkness, the sense of being lost, the fangs she'd imagined on her ankles that were palmetto cuts, the breath of some bad spirit hot on her nape. Then she had seen the glow in the dark and stumbled back to the bonfire. How delicate the ties that bind us to another. A gleam in the dark. The bell on a nurse's neck chiming. The bodies leaning in, the pressure so intense she couldn't breathe, the release.

SNAKE STORIES

====

Babe, when Satan tempted Adam and Eve, there's a pretty good reason he didn't transform into a talking clam.

It was my husband who said this to me.

This statement of his has begun to seem both ludicrous and dangerous, like the three-foot rat snake my younger son almost stepped on in the street yesterday, thinking it a stick.

Walk outside in Florida, and a snake will be watching you: snakes in mulch, snakes in scrub, snakes waiting from the lawn for you to leave the pool so they can drown themselves in it, snakes gazing at your mousy ankle and wondering what it would feel like to sink their fangs in deep.

All around us, since the fall, from the same time other terrible things happened in the world at large, marriages have been ending, either in a sort of quiet drifting away or in flames. The night my husband explicated original sin to me, we were drunk and walking home very early in the morning from a New Year's Eve party. Our host, Omar Varones, had made a bonfire out of the couch upon which his wife had cuckolded him. It was a vintage mid-century modern, and he could have sold it for thousands, but it's equally true that the flames were a stunning and unexpected soft green.

I feel like a traitor to my own when I say this, but it's wonderful to walk beside a man who is so large that nobody would mess with him, toward your own bed, at a time when everybody is sleeping save for the tree frogs and the sinners. I have missed my walks late at night, my dawn runs. Even though my neighborhood is a gem, there have been three rapes in three months within a few blocks of my house. Nights when I can't sleep, when my nerves jangle me from one son's bed to the other's, then back to my own and then out to the couch, I can even feel in my bloodstream the new venom that has entered the world, a venom that somehow acts only on men, hardening what had once been bad thoughts into new, worse actions.

———

t is strange to me, an alien in this place, an ambivalent northerner, to see how my Florida sons take snakes for granted. My husband, digging out a peach tree that had died from climate change, brought into the house a shovel full of poisonous baby coral snakes, brightly enameled and writhing. Cool! said my little boys, but I woke from frantic sleep that night, slapping at my sheets, sure their light pressure on my body was the twining of many snakes that had slipped from the shovel and searched until they found my warmth.

Other nights, my old malaria dream returns: the ceiling a twitching pale belly, sensitive to my hand. All night scales fall on me like tissue paper.

can't get away from them, snakes. Even my kindergartener has been strangely transfixed by them all year. Every project he brings home: snakes.

The pet project: *i thnk a kobra wud be a bad pet becus it wud bit me*, picture of him being eaten by a cobra.

The poetry project: *snakes eat mise thy slithr slithr slithr thy jump otof tres thy hisssssssssssssssss*, picture of a snake jumping out of a tree and onto a screaming him. Or so I assume: my child is in a minimalist period, his art all wobbly sticks and circles.

Why, of all beautiful creatures on this planet of ours, do you keep writing about snakes? I ask him.

Becus i lik them and thy lik me, he tells me.

As we walked home on New Year's morning, the night of the flaming couch, I was saying I hated the word *cuckold*, that *cuckolding* takes the woman out of the adultery and turns it into a wrestling match between the husband and the lover. A giant cockfight, if you will. Giant cockfight! my husband laughed, because there is no situation in which that phrase would not be funny to him. My husband is an almost entirely good person, and I say this as someone who believes that our better angels are matched by our bitterest devils, and there's a constant battle happening inside all of us: a giant cockfight. My husband is overrun with angels, but even he struggles with things that appeal. For instance, Omar's wife, Olivia, was the kind of shining blonde who always wore workout clothes, and my husband always gravitated toward her at parties, and they'd stand there joking and laughing into their cups for a far longer time than was conventionally acceptable between two good-looking people who were married to other people. Sometimes, when I caught his eye, my husband would wink guiltily at me while still laughing with her. After the divorce and a few uncomfortable meetings, I only ever see Olivia driving through the neighborhood while I walk the dog, and half the time I pretend I don't recognize her; I just look down and murmur something to the dog, who understands me all too well.

In February, one day, I found myself sad to the bone. A man had been appointed to take care of the environment even though his only desire was to squash the environment like a cockroach. I was thinking about the world my children will inherit, the clouds of monarchs they won't ever see, the underwater sound of the mouths of small fish chewing the living coral reefs that they will never hear.

I stood for a long time at the duck pond with my dog, who sensed she should be still and patient. The swans were on their island with the geese, and a great blue heron legged through the shallow water. I watched as the heron became a statue, then as it whipped its head down and speared something. When it lifted its beak, it held a long, thin water snake. We watched, transfixed, as the bird cracked its head down so hard three times that the snake separated in half, spilling blood. And the heron swallowed one half, which was still so alive that I could see it thrashing down that long and elegant throat.

This reminded me of the *Iliad*: *For a bird had come upon [the Trojans], as they were eager to cross over, an eagle of lofty flight, skirting the host on the left, and in its talons it bore a blood-red monstrous snake, still alive as if struggling, nor was it yet forgetful of combat, it writhed backward, and smote him that held it on the breast beside the neck, till the eagle, stung with pain, cast it from him to the ground and let it fall in the midst of the throng, and himself with a loud cry sped away down the blasts of the wind.*

This was an omen, clear and bright.

The Trojans did not heed it, and they suffered.

B ut wait. You know that the moral of Adam and Eve is that woman gets pegged with all of human sin, I told my husband that night we walked home through the dark. We were jaywalking against a red light, but there were no cars anywhere around, our own minor sin unseen.

Yet another trick of the serpent's, my husband agreed sadly.

O n the day I found the girl, the robins were migrating and the crape myrtles flashed with red.

Clouds rested their bellies atop the buildings. I went out for my run fast, because I knew rain was coming, and for a long time I have been sure that I will die one day by lightning strike. I have known this since the day when I was running across the parking lot at my older son's Montessori preschool and I leapt up the wooden steps to the door and turned around and saw a lightning bolt crash and sizzle across the slick wet blacktop where I'd just been.

I turned back when the rain crashed down and made the shadows of the woods on both sides boil. There was a shortcut behind the bed-and-breakfast district, a narrow alley with overgrown rosebushes that snatch at your clothes. I didn't see the girl until the last minute, when I had to jump her outstretched legs, and came down slant-wise on the cinders, and hit my hip and shoulder and knew immediately that they were bleeding. I rolled over, and crawled back to the girl. She stared at me darkly, and twitched her legs. She was alive, then.

I saw the rip in her T-shirt. I saw her bleeding hands, the swelling already beginning on the side of her face. And the cold place in me that I've always had, that I have carried through many dark streets in many cities, knew.

Wait here, I said, thinking I would run to a bed-and-breakfast and call the police, an ambulance, but the girl said hoarsely, No, with such panic that I looked around and saw how dark the overgrown alley was, and thick with twining vines, how a person could be hiding in many places there. Let me take you with me, and we can call the cops, I said, and she said ferociously, No fucking cops. No ambulance.

Okay, I said, and my brain had emptied out, and I said, I'll take you to my house. I'm only a few blocks away. She closed her eyes, and I took it for assent, and I helped her stand and saw the blood dissolving from her thighs in the rain.

The water was ankle deep in the roads already; the drivers had pulled off, waiting to be able to see. She was light. The side of her face next to mine was beautiful, long eyelashes, full lips, perfect skin, a sore-looking nose piercing. I helped her inside and rushed around to get towels and draped them over her and tenderly dabbed the shining drops of rain from her hair. She would not take tea. She would not let me call for help. She would not let me make her food. She just snapped, Fuck off, lady.

I fucked off. I let her sit and sat beside her in my kitchen. And when, after she stopped shaking I asked if I could please take her to the hospital, she barely spoke when she said, No. Home.

I put a towel on the passenger seat, and we drove through the empty wet streets with their dripping oaks and palms, and we came into the neighborhood between La Pasadita Grille and the Spanish church, and she said, Left, Right, Left, and Here.

After a storm, the sunlight in this town pours upward as though radiating from the ground, and the sudden beauty of the stucco and Spanish moss is a hard punch at the center of the heart.

I looked at the small green cabin in its yard of sand-spurs and neglected orange trees and rotted fruit shimmering with wasps, and everything caught the sun and shined like blessed objects. Then I saw the broken windows and the black garbage bag on the porch spilling its guts and felt the bottom drop out of my stomach. Please let me help you, I said. She said, Don't fucking say a word to anybody. And she got out of the car, slammed the door, and shuffled up the path and into the cabin.

My boys and husband were already at home. He was making dinner. That's a lot of blood, my older son said, pointing at the piles of towels on the chair. My husband was looking at me with worry in his face. I picked the towels up and backed out the door and took them with me to the police department where I described the girl, between sixteen and twenty, probably Latina, but they could or would do nothing, until one officer succumbed to my white-woman insistence and drove to the cabin with me.

It was dark by then. I watched his flashlight go up the path, the circle of light on the door growing smaller and clearer as he neared. He knocked and knocked. Then he tried the doorknob and went in. When he came to the car, he said, Looks like she had you take her to an abandoned place. And later, dropping me off at my car, he put his hand on my shoulder and said, Those people, they're like children, they have no— But I shot him a look of death and he stopped. But when I couldn't stop crying, at last in frustration he said, Listen, maybe immigration was an issue, I don't know. But lady, you can't help people who don't want your help.

On New Year's morning, my husband and I reached our house when the sky had lightened to gray in the corner. We went in. Our children were at their grandparents', but we were so tired and had been married too long to make much use of that fact. He went straight to bed without brushing his teeth. I peed in the dark, thinking about the one time Olivia and I had met up after the divorce for awkward drinks and she'd said she'd known her marriage was over when she found a snake in the toilet bowl. I know myself enough to understand that even if I suspected something, I would never look.

I stripped off my clothes and took a shower. Under the warm water, I thought about how, before I met my husband, I'd dated a nice man for a summer in Boston. He was good-looking, cried at movies, played ultimate, was a socialist, a nice guy, everyone said. One night we came home when the bars closed and both of us were drunk and I thought it was funny to shout, Help, help! I don't know this man! but it made him so angry that he stalked home ahead of me and was already in bed by the time I came into his apartment. I smelled like sweat and spilled beer and cigarette smoke, and decided to take a shower that night, too. Halfway through, I heard the curtain open and only had time to say, Wait, before he'd pushed himself into me, and I pressed my cheek against the tile and let the soap sting my eyes and breathed and counted by fives until he was done. He left. I washed myself slowly until the water went cold. He was snoring when I came into his bedroom. I stood naked and shivering for a very long time, so tired that I couldn't think, then moved and touched his dresser and opened a drawer and found a T-shirt that smelled like him and crawled under the covers to get warm enough to think again, to get it together, to go back to my own place. Instead, I fell asleep. What had happened seemed so distant when we woke up in the morning. We never talked about it. I never told anyone, not even my husband. When we broke up in a few weeks, that man dumped me.

When I came out of the bathroom, the birds were singing in the magnolia out the window and my husband was snoring. I put my wet head on his chest, and he woke up, and because he is a kind man, he hugged it and stroked my nape. My eyes were closed and I was almost asleep when I said, Tell me. You think there are still good people in the world?

Oh, yes, he said. Billions. It's just that the bad ones make so much more noise.

Hope you're right, I said, then fell asleep. But in the middle of the night, I woke and stood and checked all the windows and all the doors, I closed all the toilet lids, because, even though I was naked and the night was freezing, in this world of ours you can never really know.

YPORT

═══

The mother decides to take her two young sons to France for August.

She has been ambushed all spring by quick fits, like slaps to the heart. Where they come from, she doesn't know, but she is tired of keeling over in the soap aisle or on the elliptical or in the unlit streets where she walks her dread for hours late at night.

Also, Florida in the summer is a slow hot drowning. The humidity grows spots on her skin, pink where she is pale, pale where she is tan. She feels like an unsexy cheetah under her clothes.

These reasons seem slight. Dread and heat. None of her family or friends would understand. Anyway, since winter, they, with their worries about schools and Scouts and tenure and yoga, have seemed so distant to her, halfway dissolved in the sunset. Her work is mysterious to them, but they can understand its necessity. So they nod knowingly when she tells them she has to do research on Guy de Maupassant.

It's not untrue. For ten years, she has been stuck on a project about the writer. Or maybe Guy de Maupassant has been stuck in her, a fish bone lodged in her throat.

The problem of Guy de Maupassant is grave.

Once, during her darkest months, Guy de Maupassant had meant a great deal to her. She was eighteen and an exchange student in Nantes, France, for a year, and didn't know the language as well as she'd believed. She had been put in a *collège* into *la troisième*, a class of fourteen-year-olds. In her misery, she grew fat on crêpes and cheese, poked at her stomach in the mirror and watched it jiggle. The salvation was the cheap paperback bookstore, five francs for a book, an education one dollar at a time. The first book she bought had been a thin pale edition of Guy de Maupassant's *Contes de la Bécasse*. She skipped class to sit in the Japanese garden down by the river, where she could be hidden by a sort of grand and impersonal beauty. She loved the book, and the writer, because reading his warm voice made her feel less alone, less inept.

Slowly, through reading, she became aware of the way the demands of a language can change you. She became a different person in French: colder, more elegant, more restrained. She is most herself in French, she hopes.

With the Guy project, she wants to explode the writer or explore him, she doesn't know which. It began as a translation project, but after she read more than three hundred of his stories and found a mere handful she loved, it then turned into a historical fiction. But reimagining another writer's life in fiction has begun to seem tricksy to her, diversionary, like sleight of hand. The times are too troubled for such things. These urgent days she wants the truth, stark and cold.

Her boys take the news of going to France stoically. They do not even cry.

Her older son will be seven at the end of August. He is of a physical beauty so rare that sometimes she can't believe he'd come out of her. He is muscular, very tall for his age, with a graceful large-eyed face like a fawn's. His beauty is mitigated by painful shyness and extreme sensitivity.

He's like a perfect, windless pond, her husband once said. You throw something in just to watch it sink, and you're going to see it on the bottom staring back at you for the rest of your life.

The four-year-old is different. He is sunny, golden. He sucks his thumb, even though they paint a bitter polish on it. He carries around a cat puppet called Whoopie Pie. He makes friends with everyone. After the endless flight, during which he vibrated and did not sleep, on the train from De Gaulle to their rented apartment in the *onzième* he shows a big-boned German girl his tiny red backpack. The girl was crying, but when he climbs into her lap, sucking his thumb and reaching back to fondle the girl's ear, she clutches him to her and puts her eyes in his hair. The mother worries that he smells rancid, his skin is still covered in the milk he spilled all over himself back in Orlando, in that other, Florida life that she already doesn't regret having left behind them. But the German girl doesn't seem to mind. The mother and her sons get off the train, the older boy holding the little one's hand tightly and the mother carrying all their bags in her two strong arms. The mother looks back and sees that the solace was temporary, that the German girl has started weeping all over again.

They spend the first week in Paris because the mother is hoping the boys will pick up French the way they pick up dirt. She takes them every morning to the Poussin Vert playground in the Jardin du Luxembourg to play with French children and learn French by osmosis, but her sons keep to themselves, zip-lining over and over again, the little one trying to hold his brother's hand, his brother too sweaty and focused to allow him. They eat lunch, a decent prix-fixe vegetarian at Le Restaurant Foyot, and though it's only one o'clock, she gets buzzed on a half carafe of cold white wine and laughs too hard when she shows her boys how to eat crème brûlée.

It disconcerts her to find that Paris has become somehow Floridian, all humidity and pink stucco and cellulite rippling under the hems of shorts. It is ten degrees warmer than it should be, much brighter and louder than the Paris that lives in her memory. She had always thought this would be the place to be during the climate wars that she sees looming in the future. A city of water, surrounded by fields, temperate and contained. But maybe there is no place to be; maybe all places on a hotter planet will be equally bad, desert and hunger everywhere, even here. The mother takes her boys to do touristy things in the searing afternoons, puppet shows and Eiffel Towers and museums and picturesque early dinners on the Seine. They speak for five minutes a day with her husband over Skype, but he doesn't really have time; August is when he works eighteen hours a day, and the boys sense his impatience and become resentful and less and less willing to come to the computer to chat. When she speaks to adults, it is only to order things, her French going gluey in her head.

At night the boys sleep ten hours in the same cramped room with her. The mother, in order to have some time alone, drinks wine and watches French sitcoms on her computer with earphones. She really should be rereading Guy, or taking his biographers into the bathtub, elegant Francis Steegmuller, lascivious Henri Troyat, but she's too tired; she'll get started tomorrow. Every evening she tells herself that the next day they will go to visit Dr. Esprit Blanche's asylum, where Guy died at forty-two years old of tertiary syphilis. A century before it was a madhouse, it had been the Palais de Lamballe; the Princesse de Lamballe was Marie Antoinette's dearest friend, and when the revolutionaries came for the princess, they raped her, lopped off her head, and paraded it on a spike before the queen's window. When Guy was in his final throes of insanity, believing that there were precious jewels in his urine and that he was the son of God, the headless princess came through the walls to visit him.

Yet day after day, the mother doesn't go to Guy's last home: there would have been so much to explain to her children, what syphilis is, what insanity is, what revolutions are. Instead, every day, she wakes foggily with the boys at dawn, starving for *pain au chocolat* and coffee and fruit, and gets sucked into their life of playgrounds and joy. At last, before she can see where Guy ended his days, she runs out of time.

On the seventh day, they get up very early and take a train to Rouen, where, at the station, they rent a Mercedes for the drive west to the Alabaster Coast, in Normandy, where Maupassant was born and where he returned again and again. His mother, Laure, was from the area, a woman who gave her two sons their love of books, who went on walking tours in Europe alone as a younger woman, who dared to divorce back when divorce was not done, but who ended up a neurasthenic, sad and alone, both sons dead of syphilis, trying to strangle herself with her own long hair.

The mother drives, feeling fat and wasteful and American in the Mercedes. She has never understood the purpose of luxury cars, but she couldn't drive a stick shift on the tight cliffside roads or she would stall the car and kill them all.

The trip should take an hour, but they get lost in the twisty tiny villages, and the four-year-old pukes on Whoopie Pie, then falls asleep; and the six-year-old cries quietly to himself when she yells at him to stop whining about the smell, and she has to crack the window to settle her own stomach, and then drizzle whips incessantly into her eyes, and she pauses in Fécamp to ask directions of a man who pretends not to understand her French when she knows, irritatedly, that her French is, in fact, quite good. She is shaking when at last they swing down a steep hillside into Yport.

It is a fishing village, all silex and brick and stone streets and hills. There is a small curve of beach covered in fist-sized stones, bracketed by extreme cliffs that are disappointingly not white but creamy beige limestone with horizontal veins of gray flint. The air here, she thinks, has some kind of fizz to it, something thrilling, which makes you feel drunk, makes you want to dance and do wild things as soon as you arrive, as though you've just drunk a bottle of champagne. She's pleased with herself until she recognizes her thought as a paraphrase from Guy's best story, "Boule de Suif." She parks in the lot at the casino to await a man named Jean-Paul, who is supposed to show them to the house at three. She feels heavy when she sees on the clock that it is only eleven.

We're here! she says.

We're where? the older boy says. They look together through the windshield at the empty gray beach, the gray ocean, the gray sky overhead.

Nowhere, he says darkly.

The little boy wakes with a start and says, Flags!

She hadn't noticed, but it is true, there are two dozen flags on very tall poles lining the boardwalk, all frayed for the last foot or so at the whipping ends. Not one is American. This place is for the Swedes of the world, the Danes, the Brits, but certainly not the Americans. She is glad. When she steps out, the wind is chilly, the gulls scream overhead, but she feels a looseness in her joints, a wildness that she identifies as freedom from the doom that had waited for her just around the corner at home in Florida, that she'd even felt watching her in Paris. Yport is so small, so anonymous. It has gone downhill since Renoir painted it. Surely, her bad pet dread would never think to look for her here.

Down on the beach, the boys chunk rock after rock into the boiling waves. They like the rattle the stones make on the hard bottom in the troughs and the gulping sound the stones make in the crests. They climb into a cave in the cliff that is shaped like the nave in a church, but get spooked. She admires the way the wind tousles the older boy's dark hair, and she doesn't notice when the little one strips quickly to his underoos and runs into the rough waves. She sees only a flash of gold hair going under. She wades in and drags him out. His skin and lips are blue and his face is startled, but when the older brother laughs at him, he laughs, too.

I
t is so cold in the wind. Her skirt is wet and the little one is shuddering, but she is too tired to go back to the car to change their clothes. There is a small set of tin shacks on the beach for souvenirs, fried seafood, gelato. There, protected by a lufting sheet of clear plastic, she orders three buckwheat *galettes* with cheese and egg, and one salted caramel crêpe for dessert. At home they eat sugar only on holiday or in emergencies—she knows it is a poison; it can make you fat and crazy and eventually lose your memories when you are old, and she has a severe horror of being a stringy-haired cackler in the old-age home; she has boys, she's not dumb, she knows that sad obsolescence will more than likely be her fate if humanity even lasts that long, as girls are the ones who change your diapers when you've lost control of your bodily functions, and no son wants to wet-wipe his mother's vulva—but she wants her boys to love France and has discovered of herself that she isn't above bribery. She holds the little son against her skin,

LAUREN GROFF

under her shirt and cardigan, to warm him up. Then the
bigger one says that it isn't fair, that he is cold, too, and so
she makes room on her lap and lets him into her cardigan.
Like a bag of holding, it stretches to encompass them all.
She isn't hungry, so she drinks her local cider and lets the
alcohol warm her. It has low notes of manure and grass,
which nauseates her until she thinks of the taste as terroir.
This is what Guy de Maupassant tasted long ago, she
imagines, sitting in this same salty cold.

Of all the Guys she knows—the Parisian playboy who
seduced rich society ladies, the obscene youth rowing and
fucking on the Seine, the obsessed Mediterranean yachter
chased from harbor to harbor by his madness—she truly
loves only the Guy of the Alabaster Coast. He had been a
hearty dark-haired Norman child here, running barefoot
in the orchards and playing with the children of the fishermen. And she can imagine him on this beach as a very
young man, walking into the waves for a dawn swim.
Laughing, his moustaches dripping, red in the cheeks.
This Guy who was as strong as a bull, not yet a bad man.

Atop the cliffs, there are emerald meadows of grass
blown back by the wind like pompadours. There are tiny
white specks that she squints to see. Cows or sheep? she
asks the boys, and they make fun of her terrible eyesight
and finally say, Sheep, Mommy, jeez, definitely sheep.

She holds them in her arms and sniffs their necks and
imagines one iconoclastic sheep, after a long life of envy-
ing the birds in their graceful rest above the sea, coming

to a sudden decision. He'd take a step to turn gloriously bird. Then he'd meet the ocean, turn jellyfish.

When the boys finish their food and hers, they slide to the ground. Her dark green cardigan is stretched hopelessly out of shape, streaked in yellow with yolk.

The boys jump off a low stone wall in front of the casino into a bed of lavender orbited by golden bees. She thinks of herself as a mother who lets her children make their own mistakes. She doesn't want the boys to be in pain, but she wouldn't mind if they began to pay more attention to danger, and the world is full of far worse lessons than a bee sting.

Now a stocky sixty-year-old man is coming down the hill, hallooing. This can only be Jean-Paul. His face is windbattered. If he has eyes, they are so deep and hooded by his shaggy brows she can't see them. His odor shakes her hand before his hand does, some combination of unwashed clothes, body, salt, breath. He smells like a lifelong bachelor.

He apologizes for being so late, says the house is ready, that they are going to be very happy there. He is surprised at her French, he says. It isn't bad! He says he has a gift for her, that the guy who owns the house has told him that she was researching Guy de Maupassant, and . . . He pulls out a wad of paper from the back pocket of his jeans and unfolds it dramatically before giving it to her.

LAUREN GROFF

She looks at it. He's printed out for her the French
Wikipedia page for Guy de Maupassant: Henri René
Albert Guy de Maupassant, b. 5 August 1850, d. 6 July
1893, protégé of Flaubert, failed suicide, Naturalist writer
of short stories and novels, et cetera. Jean-Paul waits. She
swallows her laugh, says it is very nice of him to do that,
and that he shouldn't have, and thanks very much. This is
apparently insufficient. He frowns and squints at her,
then turns and takes the boys' hands. The older boy lets
him hold his for just long enough to not be rude, then
takes it away, but the little one keeps holding the hand
and chats with Jean-Paul, despite the odor and mutual
incomprehension. They start up a very long flight of
stairs, seventy-four steps, she'll count later, carved into
the steep hillside. The mother carries all three of the bags,
which are heavy.

The older boy hangs back with her and says quietly
that he doesn't like that man, that he is stinky and there is
something weird about him.

Oh, he's not so bad, she tells him. She is wheezing a
little. At the top, Jean-Paul and the little boy have turned
around and are watching her power upward, step by step.

Jean-Paul laughs and calls down that she reminds him
of a she-goat.

Changed my mind, Monkey, she murmurs to her
older boy, I don't like him, either.

Atop the hill, the streets are nervous, haphazard, full
of short jogs up a half step and quick alleys. Everything is

made of stone. In the sun, out of the wind, it is quite warm. Red geraniums spill everywhere.

At last, Jean-Paul drops the little boy's hand, pulls out a key with a flourish, opens a door in a wall beside other doors, and steps in. He says that here they are, here's home. Inside, it is sparse, which suits her, all rock and wood and white plaster, three rooms stacked atop one another, connected by a spiral staircase. Someone's grandmother's furniture. There is a fatty, rotting smell that she recognizes from an apartment in Boston when she was young, a few weeks of low-level anguish after a rat died in the walls. There is a table, chairs, a couch and television downstairs, a trundle bed and a bathroom on the next floor, and at the top her tiny white room with only a queen-sized bed in it. There is dirt on the windowsills, long hairs and sand in the drains.

The two skylights in her own bare white room at the top are open, and she sticks her head through. On one side, she sees only sky, the daydreaming sheep above the cliffs. But the other is full of slate rooftops shining like damp skin. Everything she sees from here is striped: the red-and-tan clock tower at the center of town, the roofs of the blue-and-white tin cabanas on the beach, the creamy cliffs with their veins of flint, the ocean's navy with whitecaps, the tiny people walking the boardwalk in their mariner's shirts. The wind is raw on her cheeks.

She brings her head back in. Jean-Paul is standing very close. His scent is strong, and it combines with the dead-animal smell from the kitchen to become somehow an unpleasant film in her mouth.

He wants to show her how to use the television, the wifi, the stovetop, but she says, No, no. Thank you! No, no, no, no. She goes down the stairs, over and over thanking Jean-Paul, who is following her. From the front door, she calls up for the boys, who are leaping off the bed and making the house shake as they land. They come down grumblingly. She has to go grocery shopping, she says; it is imperative. If there are problems, she'll get in touch with the owner. It is great to meet Jean-Paul. She opens the door. He hangs back. She says goodbye three different ways. He slinks out. She opens all the windows and waits for ten minutes as the wind blows the last of him out, then when she is sure he is gone, she makes the boys put their sandals on again.

The mean-mouthed woman at the town's only *épicerie* laughs at the mother when she tries to fit all the groceries into the reusable bag she brought from Florida. The mother feels ashamed: she saw an excellent burgundy at an astonishing price, one fifteenth of what the wine would have cost in the United States, and bought all four bottles on the shelf. They make the cardboard box the woman gives her heavy.

The boys pass the bakery slowly, sniffing. They speed by the butcher shop because the window is gruesome with dead flesh. They are vegetarians, though only when it comes to creatures with faces.

It was simple to get to the center of town, but now the mother appears to have lost her way. The streets were silent and eerie with drizzle when they arrived in the morning but are now thronging with visitors. The boys run ahead; she yells to prevent them from being hit by the cars sliding along in the tight roads between the houses. They look back at her blankly.

She asks someone where their street is, but the man, clearly a fisherman, responds in an impossible French, a French that makes her fear she has somehow lost her French entirely. Yportais, she'll learn later, is its own dialect, as knotty as old rope.

At last she puts down the groceries and rubs her arms. She won't cry, she tells herself firmly. The older boy has found a tall round pole beside a set of stairs leading up to a bricked-in front door. He is showing his little brother how to climb up, slide down. Dark hair, gold hair, dark, then gold.

Guy was also the beloved older brother of someone smaller and blonder, Hervé. But Hervé was the even more tragic mirror of his tragic brother, and the parallel feels like a curse on her own boys, and she rushes it out of her mind.

The littlest playground in the world! her sons shout, sliding.

She watches, feeling each slide in her own body. She

had a battery-operated toy when she was little, a set of penguins that marched up a staircase only to launch down a curvy slide and start the march again. The thrill was vicarious, the adrenaline outsourced. Good training, the mother thinks, for a life in books.

She comes up the sidewalk, pushing the box with her feet.

What's wrong, Mommy? the little one says.

I think we're lost, she says. Don't worry. I'll figure it out.

He makes a pinched face as if he'd sucked a lemon, then slides down the pole and runs up the stairs again.

The older boy comes over and stands on her feet, pressing his head into her sternum. He looks up at her face questioningly. Isn't that it? he says, pointing to a great cracked terra-cotta pot with red geraniums, beside which is the gap in the houses that leads into their narrow street. He knew where they were for a while but was being careful of her feelings, she sees. Sweet child. Or not so sweet, because when they arrive at the house, while she fumbles with the key, the older boy either pushes his little brother off the step or doesn't mean to knock him off, it is hard to tell; he has gone watchful in his graceful predator's body, but the little one's wails are echoing in the close street and his knee has a dab of blood on it, and she hustles all three inside as quickly as she can and shuts the door against their noise, for fear of the neighbors.

———

She cleans the house while the boys play with Legos, though the place was supposed to have been already cleaned before they arrived; this is why they had to wait until the afternoon to see it. There is nothing she can do about the smell but keep the windows open and hope for a speedy decay. They eat pasta and carrots, and go for a walk before bed, and on the way home there are cooking odors, people just beginning their evenings in vacationland, the sun still bright overhead.

She sings the boys the Magnetic Fields' "Book of Love" and reads to them from *The Little Prince*, and they fall asleep quickly in their sleeping bags because they can't understand French and she might as well have been singing whalesong. Oh, but she loves the language in her mouth, the silk and bone of it, the bright vowels and the beautiful shapes a mouth makes to speak it.

Downstairs, people keep passing the window, and their voices are loud. She closes it, closes the curtain. The wifi won't work, though she turns the router on and off many times, though she follows the instructions in the binder the house owner left, each time more carefully than the last. She isn't going to talk to her husband; he is in the thick of work by now, would respond curtly, would hurt her feelings and make her feel unloved, but maybe she has some good email, she doesn't know. She opens her notebook but finds it impossible to write. She opens a bottle of the great cheap burgundy and is startled when she goes to pour another glass to find the bottle empty so soon. There must be an invisible her in the room, drinking from the same bottle, a second her, in yoga pants and a fleece jacket and smudged glasses, a doppelgänger just like her, right next to her, but unseeable. The only explanation.

Maybe she's imagining this because Guy's later stories had many doubles, because, as Guy's disease progressed, he began seeing a ghost of himself. One of his many lovers was Gisèle d'Estoc, bisexual, a demimondaine, famous for a bare-breasted public swordfight with a female lover who wronged her. She had such a fiery temper, she was suspected of bombing Le Restaurant Foyot to get back at a nasty critic. In her posthumous tell-all about her love affair with Guy, *Cahier d'Amour*, Gisèle says that he once told her about his double:

Guy, she says, was lying still on the bed so that she could hardly see him in the shadows. The dark corners seemed to pulse with phantoms. Was he asleep? Suddenly, she heard his muted, jerky voice, saying in a harsh tone, This is the third time he's come to stop me in my work. At first he had a strange moving face, a face from a dream, my own face, as if I were looking in a mirror. This time, he wouldn't speak to me. On the last visit, this visitor who looks more like me than my own brother seemed real to me. He walked into my office and I heard his footsteps. Then he sat in my chair, all naturally, as if he belonged there. After he left, I would have sworn that he'd moved my books, my papers, all the objects on my desk. Like the last time, just now he said nothing to me, his face in an expression that has nothing to do with my work or worries. Only on this third visit did I understand what my double was thinking. He's furious with me, he hates and scorns me. And do you know why? He believes that he is the author of my books! He is accusing me of stealing them from him!

Sometimes, Guy whispered to her, I feel madness rolling around in my brain.

The mother finishes the second bottle of wine. The page before her is still blank.

Fuck it, she thinks, it is the travel, the strain of newness, the stink in the house, and her body feels heavy, as if over the course of the day it had been stuffed full of stones from the beach, all of these things conspiring to keep her from working. With some effort, she climbs the spiral staircase up into her cold white windy room.

Ten at night and yet the sun is still blazing in the skylights. She pokes her head through into the air and sees the tide far out, the black exposed seabed terrifying in its rawness, its gleam somehow sinister like the surface of a dark moon. Tiny people pick their way across it, holding white things she imagines are buckets.

On the next rooftop there is a line of seagulls. They are strangely still, facing away from her and toward the sea. She counts a dozen but stops counting because something makes her uneasy about their silence. This is a species of bird that is never quiet; they are three-fourths scream, they are the birds of rage, all of them mothers; even the male gulls are mothers.

Something, she thinks, is wrong.

Soon, pink and navy spread across the sky, and the sun blazes, then goes out. She'd read of sailors at sea who, on extremely clear days, see a flash of green the moment the sun sets. The only thing she sees is the ghost of the old dead sun on her eyelids when she closes them.

A moment later, the biggest seagull opens its wings. All at once the birds break into shrieks, laughter, wild flapping; it is deafeningly loud, and she is so startled she hits her head on the skylight, and when she stops wincing, the seagulls are lifting up in the wind, peeling off the rooftop, carrying backward toward her. She ducks again and watches a handful float backward close over her head, their tongues darting out of their open mouths like long and pink and panicked worms.

Then they are gone, their noise coming down from the distant air. She is shaking, but maybe she is just cold.

She gets into bed to warm up and within a few breaths is asleep.

n the morning, there is a tiny freezing body climbing under her warm duvet, then another one. The boys fidget but stay quiet, all elbows and knees knocking her sides, cheeks on her arms and chest. They watch the sky lighten overhead. She hadn't shut the windows and the room is frigid, the way her bedroom had been frigid when she was small and her family lived in a drafty antique house in upstate New York, and some nights she'd watch wind through a crack whip a thin string of snow across the room to settle in a tiny perfect nipple in the fireplace.

At the bakery, she makes the boys order what they want in French, and the baker looks at the mother kindly and holds her hand for a moment when she passes over the paper twists of pastries, and all the way home, the mother feels the baker's warm fingers on hers.

Not many other people are awake in Yport. A man bullying his spaniel down the street. The fishermen winching their boats with the long chains down the beach and through the channel.

Here it is, the France the mother loves. The butter and pastry in the mouth, the cobblestones, the picturesque dawn with almost no French people in it.

Today they will visit Étretat. Guy de Maupassant had loved Étretat. His mother, Laure Le Poittevin, spent most of her life there. Guy grew up there, and built a house not far from his mother's when he made money. He called it La Guillette, the little Guy, in his complacent narcissism.

The mother drives the windy road up to the top of the cliffs, which finally seem white in the morning sun, blindingly so. Aha, she thinks. It just gets dirty as it goes through the day, like the rest of us. Wow, breathes the little boy, but the elder holds his own counsel, watching. Something in him, she knows, wants her to spin the wheel and accelerate over the cliff, just to see what would happen.

Tiny forests, meadows, songbirds, villages. The Mercedes purrs into Étretat; they park on rue Guy-de-Maupassant.

The town is spotlit by the early sun, utterly still. From the density of souvenir shops, she knows it will later be full of tourists. The boys are hungry again, and she finds another bakery and again lets them have what they want as long as they order in French. Both boys choose a *salambo*, some sort of éclair with green frosting, which looks disgusting, but then again *Salammbô* the novel is her least favorite of Flaubert's books, and it seems right that the boys choose something gesturing at Flaubert, who was Guy de Maupassant's mentor and friend. Such a tragedy, to follow up the greatness of *Madame Bovary* with melodramatic historical fiction about ancient Carthage, as if a maker of an uncannily humanoid robot decided next to turn his attention to cuckoo clocks.

But Flaubert had loved Guy truly, finding in the boy the ghost of his closest friend, Alfred Le Poittevin, Guy's uncle. Alfred had been a poet who died too young, and Flaubert never got over the shock of it. When Guy grew up, he became close to Flaubert and pressed himself into Flaubert's mold: disciplined on the page and obscene in the life. Guy was called by the family to prepare and dress Flaubert's body when the master died of apoplexy; Guy wept in anger when the hole dug for the corpse was too short for the coffin. Later, a grieving Guy wrote to Turgenev: The great old soul is following me. His voice haunts me. His sentences are in my ears, his love, which I look for and can't find because it is gone, has made the entire world seem empty around me.

The mother and the boys go out to the boardwalk. The red flags are up, which means bathing is a no-go, as if anyone sane would brave these waves, wild and crashing white. This beach is like Yport's, only supersized. Here, though, the great cliffs take her breath away. On the left side, there is a needle, one huge pointed rock, as well as a giant's archway somehow carved out of the bone-white stone; on the right, a smaller archway has a church like a brown *chapeau* up top.

When they grow too cold in the wind, they walk the town, but something about the aesthetics of the buildings feels off to her, close and mean. There are brown timbers everywhere, tight streets, second and third stories that tilt frighteningly far off their foundations into the road. The native style seems so ornate and dark and airless that the effect is almost disdainful. She feels the buildings leaning like women watching behind her back, whispering.

She takes the children to the villa Les Verguies, where, after their parents' divorce, Guy and Hervé were raised by their suffering mother, but there is nothing to see there, and a great gate blocks the way. She takes the children down the long road to La Guillette. The only thing to see there is a sign that says La Guillette. She takes a picture of it, then of the boys in front of it, and then, not finding herself capable of trespass, they walk back. Some writer named Maurice Leblanc was a much bigger deal in Étretat than Guy de Maupassant, it appears; he'd written some detective named Arsène Lupin. The arsenic wolf; the name could be applied to Guy, who had taken arsenic among many other medications for his syphilis and was predatory sexually, reportedly able to make himself erect at will.

She walks her boys up the long climb toward the church atop the cliff. She carries the little one when he grows too tired to go on, and feels her muscles burn pleasantly. When she's too tired, the older boy carries his brother for a spell, and, God, this makes her want to cry with love. Up at the stone church, she stands closest to the drop like a sheepdog to keep her boys from nearing the lip of the cliff but lets them run and play around the church, climbing the steps, leaping down.

They drift down and eat a margarita pizza for lunch. They buy water shoes for the painful stones on the beaches, a mat so they can sunbathe, floaties, their own blue-and-white mariner's sweatshirts because cold like this was impossible to imagine in the hellmouth that is summer in Florida. They buy a postcard for the boys' father that will remain in the bottom of her bag, staining and shredding at the corners, unwritten, until they are home.

There is nothing else to do so they walk down, across the boardwalk, up to the top of the other cliff, where there is a staircase carved into the rock and a winding pathway with no guardrail to keep people from tripping and falling three hundred feet into the evil.

Ow, says the older boy, trying to rip his hand away from hers, but she won't let him go.

Keep me safe, she says to give him a job, pretending to be afraid. I don't want to fall.

Then both boys hold her hands and steer her around rocks and talk to her in the gentle voices she heard them use once to urge a baby gosling out of a gutter, which they tried to do for hours, until the chick got hungry and darted out and they caught him and released him into their neighborhood's duck pond, where he was never seen again, where, she thinks now, he was probably eaten immediately by a hawk, as he had no mother goose to protect him.

When they cross a narrow bridge over a vast drop, the wind nearly blows the sunglasses off her face, and she becomes genuinely frightened. She squeezes her sons' hands, having visions of their shirts filling with wind, pushing them up and into the air like kites, their little faces first dazzled and delighted and then the slow dawn of dread as they begin to blow away. She would tether them here, to the earth, with her body.

I'm not scared, the smaller boy says, pressing close to her leg.

Me neither, the older one says.

Mommy's scared, the smaller boy says. Though we're not.

Oh, Mommy's scared of everything, the older one says, but pets her leg with his free hand.

From here, the other cliff they climbed earlier shows itself to be perilous, the church ready to fall off in a gust of wind. She can't believe she let her boys run around up there. The nausea rises in her throat. She has dragged her children across the world; she is risking their death, and for what? For a long-dead writer whom she finds morally repugnant, whose work she likes only about five percent of, filled as it is with white male arrogance and anti-Semitism and misogyny and flat-out celebrations of rape.

This town, from up here, feels malevolent, an outgrowth of Guy's bad heart.

The nausea stays until they descend and she finds the car. She drives out of Étretat with a sense of relief, and the boys fall asleep, and she reads a book, parked in the casino lot back in Yport, because her boys are too beautiful, asleep like this; she can't disturb them when there's such peace in their faces.

At the end of the boardwalk in Yport, near the spooky cave in the cliff, there is a carousel of ersatz Disney characters with vehicles that jerk eight feet into the air when the boys push a button.

The woman who sold the mother twenty tickets is beautiful, a bleached blonde with huge tits. She lives in a trailer behind the carousel with a fleshy man who never wears a shirt. She never speaks. The mother thinks she is maybe Eastern European. The woman makes savage faces at the backs of the parents who buy tickets, and when she goes around to take the same tickets from the children before their rides, she rips them nastily out of their little hands.

The boys ride together in the Dumbo car. They flash by, flash by, flash by, first low then high in the air, shouting with joy over the Spice Girls.

At her first family, in a village outside Nantes, during her study-abroad year, her fourteen-year-old host sister would play the same song loudly and on repeat when her eighteen-year-old boyfriend, who was in the navy and wore a silly pom-pom on his beret, came over and they locked the door. She could hear their moaning even through the noise. *I'll tell you what I want, what I really really want*; the mother associates the song with statutory rape.

When her children descend from the air and the ride settles, the little one runs to her, banging his golden head into her lap, and only then does she understand that he is weeping; he hadn't been laughing, he'd been screaming with terror the entire time. It hadn't been the height, she understands, but the red button. His brother had told him that if the four-year-old touched it, the Dumbo would explode.

I promise you, Little Bear, she says. It won't explode.

But what if there was a bomb? he sobs.

She has committed herself to truth; she has to find a way to tell it, so she says, Well, yes, if there was a bomb, it'd explode. But who would bomb a children's carousel?

Nobody? he says.

You said it, she says.

It's true that the world is overrun with terrorists. It's true that the mother no longer goes to movies in theaters, and she scans for the exits in restaurants. Deeper, worse, the death everywhere, the surgical strikes, the eyes in the sky. Aleppo in the beautiful before, the ravaged after. She puts these thoughts away. If she could, she'd spend the entire day in bed.

Her little boy looks at her, wanting more.

I'd chase down the guy who tried to bomb you and punch him in the face, she says. Also, the penis.

You couldn't, he says, but he is laughing; the word *penis* is inherently ridiculous, the concept of a penis is ludicrous, it always gets a laugh.

Who's faster, Daddy or me? Who wins when we race at the park?

You, he says grudgingly.

There you go, she says. I'm the toughest mother in the world. I won't let anybody hurt you, she says, and she is either lying or not, it is hard to tell, because this promise is so complicated, the future so dark.

Sunset is still three hours away but the sky is pink, and the quickest way to happiness is sugar, so she buys them all ice creams. Chocolate for her, rum raisin for the boys. They sit in an upturned fishing boat to eat.

The boys vibrate until their engines shut off one after the other, and she carries one on her back, the other on her front, huffing all the way home.

She puts them to bed upstairs and doesn't bother to turn on the lights in the house. She likes the gloomy dim through the curtains downstairs. She also wants to steer clear of the seagulls, the way they shouted down the sunset the day before.

She looks at her empty notebook until its emptiness is

seared into her brain, and then she opens one bottle of burgundy and drinks it and then opens a second, because why not.

The neighbors are having dinner in their courtyard. She imagines it full of bougainvillea, bird feeders, a long antique table. Silverware that's heirloom silver but mismatched. They are talking about the migrants from the war in Syria. She has to concentrate: their French is rapid-fire and muffled with food.

An infestation, someone says. Someone else chuckles. Disgusting, those Arabs, do you see the way they treat their women? someone says. Stone them to death if some uncle molests them. Sell them off to be fucked by old men when they're eight years old. Barbaric.

She finishes the second bottle and tries the wifi again but there is none, and she can't figure out the television and the books she brought are full of Guy and she is in no mood for his bullshit tonight, not after dealing with Étretat.

She'll go to bed, she decides. She stands. But her eye falls on the door, and she sees in the glass behind the curtain the silhouette of a man. His arm is moving.

Maybe she hasn't locked the door, she thinks. She can't remember. She is pretty sure she hasn't.

She holds her breath, and her body goes into a crouch behind the sofa. There is a single soft knock on the door, and she listens to the silence afterward.

She stares at the knob, a curled lever, and keeps seeing

it move, but the movement is in her eyes, not in the knob; the knob stays where it is.

After a while, the man moves away. There is an elaborate whistling, sharp footsteps. The neighbors' voices have lowered, and she can no longer understand them. She no longer wants to listen.

She locks the door, then puts one of the kitchen chairs under the handle. She shuts all the windows. Her children's faces in the darkness are featureless pale blots. She stands over them until one complains in his sleep about the hallway light, then she crawls up the spiral to her bedroom, where there is still sun in the skylight, which she blocks out by pulling her duvet over her head.

All night she wakes with a start to see an outline in the middle of the floor, which always turns out to be her own dress drying on the back of a chair as soon as she fumbles her glasses onto her face, and at last she gives up and just sleeps with them on, and in the morning she has a pink welt from temple to ear that is tender and aches to the touch.

After three days, they brave the water. The cold is not terrible, at least as soon as breath returns. Refreshing! she shouts, coaxing the boys in, until they start saying Refreshing! to describe all the mildly unpleasant things they have to bear before they get to have any fun. Their evening warmish shower over the gritty tile. The mushy buttery carrots and peas she bought only because the jar was beautiful. Pasta again, as vegetarianism is tough in this town. The long wait in the morning until the *boulangerie* opens at dawn.

After every dip, they huddle together under the wicking travel towels she brought and wait to stop shivering.

The older boy, who has taken to reading *Astérix* in the tin shack that is a free library, makes a menhir of the beach stones. These stones, she learned, are called *galets*. She likes best the chalk ones that look like bone cracked open to reveal gray flint marrow inside.

The little boy wanders over to a girl his age, making friends as usual.

The mother lets the sun shine on her spotted skin. Every once in a while, she checks in on her younger son, then goes back to dozing. There is something not right with her head, as if in sleep a cloud had descended through her ears and now refused to burn off in the sun.

The last time she checks on the little boy, he has moved away from the girl in her silly ruffled suit and is talking to the parents.

She stands to fetch him back. The other parents are British, she hears, when she comes close. The woman is dark-haired, gamine, emphatic. The father is charming, with a jaw too big for his head. They both wear such tiny swimsuits that the mother has difficulty looking them in the face. She hasn't spoken more than a few non-commerce-related sentences to an adult in so long that she is also having trouble coming up with something to say.

She stands there in silence for a few breaths longer than is normal.

Hullo, the father says at last. Your boy is entertaining us.

Hi. That's him, she says. The entertainer. I hope he wasn't bothering you.

Not at all! the dark-haired woman says. He's a funny little one. He asked us an interesting question. He asked us if time will stop when the universe stops expanding.

The mother has to think about it. Will it? she says.

Space-time is a single fabric. Just warp and woof, the man says.

So. The answer is yes? the mother says, but the other two just smile, whitely.

The mother waits for them to say more, but when they don't, she says, Weird question for a four-year-old, for sure. I wonder where it came from.

Oh, the father says. I told him that I'm an astrophysicist. Four-year-olds tend not to know what that means, so I just said that I study space. Stars and black holes and things, I said.

I don't know what an astrophysicist does, the mother says jokingly, but the couple look at each other. Then she wants to say that, oh, Christ, of course she knows, the condescension Europeans shower on Americans is not always warranted; she's a novelist, which is tantamount to

being a one-woman card catalogue for useless knowledge. She could teach them a thing or two. But she knows
she'd sound even more pathetic to these two silky people
than she already has. The three adults watch in silence as
the children go back to their game, which involves using
gray stones to smash the chalk off white ones.

She thinks she could perhaps salvage the situation; she
has ideas of being invited over to their house for teatime,
scones and clotted cream and the children running
around their garden in search of something ineffable—
ghosts, fairies, the last gasps of cultural imperialism—and
so she introduces herself and says that she and her boys are
in Yport because she is researching Guy de Maupassant
for a writing project.

A writer, for a certain layer of society, is catnip. Apparently not this layer. They don't offer her their names.
Instead, the father says, Oh, is *that* it. We were wondering
how you ever came to be here. We've holidayed in Yport
for ten summers straight and had yet to meet an American until today.

Not missing much, the mother jokes. But he says,
Indeed!

She gives up. She calls the little boy's name and says it
is time to go up to the house for lunch. He hands his
hammer stone to the little girl, who takes it gravely.

You know, the other woman says in a low voice, tent-
ing her eyes with her hand against the sun. Your little boy
seems a bit anxious. Of course, you must be aware.

Anxious? the mother says, surprised; her youngest son is so full of light. Not this one, she says. She gestures at her other boy, scowling in concentration, his stone sculpture larger than he is. I mean, the older one, for sure, but this little guy's pretty happy, she says.

Oh? the father says. You know him best. It's simply that he asked us what would happen if a tsunami came in the middle of the night.

We said we hoped very much a tsunami wouldn't come! the other woman says.

Then we explained that most of the houses are well above the average sea-surge level and that in all likelihood, only the boardwalk and carousel and some of the restaurants would be underwater, the father says. But nobody lives at sea level, we said. So nobody would be hurt.

The children would wake up in the morning to crabs and starfish on their front steps! the other woman says.

An adventure. No need for alarm. Right, Ellie? the father says, looking at his little girl, who gives him a pinched smile, then a sigh.

The mother says goodbye but thinks, Fuck you and your space-time, too, as she picks up her perfectly lovely and gentle and normal son. He wraps himself around her torso. She backs away. The bad feeling in her lasts until they reach the house, where the garbage has been taken from the cans, but the glass, all the wine bottles, the jars, have been set out on the step. There is no room for the mother to stand to put the key in the door. Her face burns. Once they are in, she starts up a movie on the iPad even though the boys haven't asked for one yet, and puts all of the glass in plastic sacks, and hides them behind the bookshelf near the front door. She doesn't think her boys have noticed, but when she finishes and turns from the sink, drying her hands, the older boy is watching her through a part in his bangs.

She is drinking champagne out of the bottle. It tastes better that way, bubblier and colder, and after a week here, she wants the cold all the way inside her, to the center of her bones.

Down at the little cluster of tin shacks beside the boardwalk, a band is playing not-bad cover versions of the Eagles, Led Zeppelin, and Pink Floyd, though the singer's accent makes the words go rubbery and bounce.

The sunset is so excessive it fills her with nostalgia. A hot burn, everything shot red, even the skins of the slate roof tiles. The color feels like youth.

One by one the seagulls line up on the opposite peak. The giant seagull flaps to a stop on the chimney and basks there in the light.

They're just birds, she tells herself.

In the long row of gulls, there is a mangy tiny one at the center. It struggles its shoulders against its neighbors, too skinny to be at ease like the rest of the birds.

They've gone quiet again. And she doesn't know what she is watching at first when the seagull to the left of the mangy one seems to bow its head at the shivering thing, and then the one to the right does, both of them bowing and bowing. Perhaps the little one is some kind of prince bird, perhaps they are paying their respects, she thinks, confused, and then the other seagulls nearby move in on the bowing, and only then does she understand that they aren't bowing, they are killing the skinny tiny gull, pecking it to death.

Surely, if she hurls the bottle at them they'll stop. But she has frozen, and the murder is over so quickly, a heap of bloody feathers that slides out of view.

It has all been done in silence, though a high buzzing has risen to her ears from inside. The little seagull didn't even scream; it accepted meekly, it seemed to offer itself to the others. Surely it had a right, at least, to a scream. Even if it couldn't avoid the outcome, it had the luxury of protest.

The band on the boardwalk has slid into Kashmir.

I am a traveler of both time and space: I yam at raveler of boat I'm and spice.

She winches the skylights shut, puts plugs in her ears and presses pillows against them, and the furling music and the sudden screaming of the seagulls at the loss of the sun becomes only a small hubbub at the very center of her brain, where the heat pulses on and on, and won't stop.

The road curves, and as it does, the mass of cornstalks chest-high in the fields separates into clear rows, as if a comb has passed through. Deeper into the curve, the corn masses together again.

The boys want to talk to their father in Florida. It has been more than a week. She keeps meaning to fix the wifi or ask the owner to do so, but she keeps being distracted. It is early in the morning, five-thirty in Florida, but August means that her husband works from dawn to midnight, and even if she and her boys had been in the house, they'd have been an irritation to him. She knows her husband will be awake by now and worrying his coffee.

They are going to the giant Carrefour up the road, a kind of massive grocery store with a cheese store, an in-house optometrist, a media section, a café. Surely, they will offer wifi. She can buy prepackaged meals; she is growing tired of what she could make with the single saucepan and skillet at the house. She can buy DVDs in French for the boys. She can buy wine so the lady at the épicerie won't twist her tight lips in and out and look at the mother calculatingly when she rings up the bottles. She can buy socks, because she brought none for her sons and their sandals add a new thick layer of stink to the house. An invasive species from America, the megastore.

Once inside, she tries Skype on her phone, but it trills and trills and her husband doesn't answer.

Where is he? the little one says.

Out running! she says brightly. She buys them a *chausson aux pommes* to share.

Up the aisles. Jam, brioche, eggs, cheese.

Down the aisles. Wine, pickles, packaged carrot salad, fruit. It is comforting, this cleanness, the neatness here.

They try again and again and again, bleeping until the call trails off.

In the backseat, the older boy stares at his hands.

What's wrong, Monkey? she says.

He doesn't want to talk to us, he says in a low voice.

That's not true, she says. He loves you. He's always happy to talk to you.

Then he doesn't want to talk to you.

That's not it, either. She thinks quickly. He's probably out for breakfast. You know he won't make himself breakfast if we're not around.

Not even cereal? the older boy says skeptically.

He's probably skinny, she says. Wasted. A skeleton of his previous self.

No. I bet he eats burritos like three times a day, the older boy says, and he brightens. I bet he's superfat. Like when we get home, we won't even know who he is. He's smooshing out of his clothes.

I bet he's dead, the little boy says. He gives a little chuckle.

Hey! That's not nice, she says.

I didn't say I *wanted*, I said I *bet*, the little one says.

I bet he's at Bill and Carol's right now, the older boy says. I bet he has an omelet and a stack of pancakes and a biscuit with butter and honey and toast and coffee and orange juice and hash browns, and is just like shoving it all in like a steam shovel. It's like falling all out of his mouth.

Yuck, the little boy says.

And a milkshake and a banana split and vegan chocolate cake and corn nuggets and a tempeh Reuben and french fries and hot sauce. And lobster soup and baked potatoes and broccoli and bean tacos.

When her bigger boy is like this, almost smiling, she wants to fold his triangular fawn's face in her hand and keep it warm there forever.

The little boy throws up into his lap.

In the morning, the glass bottles are again on the steps, so many, ghosts of her nights. Someone is trying to tell her something. She heaps them inside, behind the front door. The pile makes her desperate.

There is too much noise and fog in her head to leave the house all morning, and she lets the boys stay in their pajamas after breakfast and they watch *Tintin*.

She feels obligated to attend to Guy. She can't bear the biographies, the sour ugly man in them makes her feel sick, so she returns to the Guy she likes, the young man who wrote her favorite of his stories, "Histoire d'une Fille de Ferme." The prose is beautiful, simple. It begins with a servant girl on a farm, on a torpid day, going out to a sweet-smelling little hollow full of violets to take a nap.

As the mother reads, she can almost see Guy's square young face in the open window; it is 1881, Étretat, a relatively warm day in early March. There are carriage and seabird sounds coming into the room. Papers breathe under the stone weight. Guy touches his moustache nervously with his tiny callused hand, dreaming a fiction into life, a farm girl lying back in her damp hollow, sex stirring in her body. Inside Guy, the imagined girl is being made real; in the mother's imagining of him, Guy is also being made real.

Now the boys run over to her because *Tintin* has ended. The little boy farts, then raises a finger into the air like a gun and says, *Un pistolet!*

When they finally go down to the beach, they find the tide all the way withdrawn, a wasteland of black and green, and the older boy says, in Captain Haddock's voice, *Mille milliards de mille sabords.*

They sit anyway, out of the wind at the pop-up free library. The teenager who watches them, day after day, lets them be. The mother finds Marguerite Duras and Michel Houellebecq and J. M. G. Le Clézio, and the boys flip through *bandes dessinées*, and she reads and ignores the shelf of Maupassant staring down at her.

She starts *Moderato Cantabile*, a book that has always struck her as contemptible, too cynical to be believed. There is no love in the book, not even in the mother character for her smart and naughty son.

From time to time, she looks up at the tiny figures picking at the edges of the receding tide, then back at her book to read.

The sun grows warmer. She takes off her jacket.

There is something beating louder in her, behind her thoughts and the book's taut words, something terrible, but she can't look at it, she needs to look away; if she looks at it, it will come even closer to her, rub up against her, and she can't let it, all alone in this cold place with her two small boys to care for.

The big boy sits on her feet and leans his dark head against her knees. The wind plays with his hair, but he won't let her touch him. After a while, she feels his body stiffen. The little boy says, It's my friend!

She sees the galoshes in front of her, the jeans patched at the knees, the belly jutting over the belt. Jean-Paul. He is grinning and his teeth are thick at the gum with tartar. The little boy is waving Whoopie Pie at him.

Alors! Jean-Paul says. He thought it was them from way out, he came in to say hi, to see how the researches were going, how the boys liked this little town, if the house was treating them right, if all was well, if there was anything he could do to make her more comfortable.

She says it is all fine, fine, fine. She thinks of the

broken wifi, but doesn't want Jean-Paul in the house and stays silent about it.

He stares at her, or she thinks he does, his eyes so sunken. He shows the boys his bucket. There are shells moving slowly in it. He tells her they're *bulots*.

At first, she translates this in her head as jobs, *boulots*, which makes no sense. Then she understands the creatures to be whelks. Sea snails. Escargot from the sea.

The little one dandles his hand in the bucket happily, but the older one makes a polite noise and leans harder into his mother's legs.

There is not much left to say. Jean-Paul offers them some whelks, and she tells him no thanks! and then he makes jokes with the boys that they don't understand, and when the silence goes on too long, he crunches away. They watch him pick over the black mottled rock.

Were those alive? the older boy says.

Yes, she says. People eat them with garlic and butter.

Oh, the little boy says, then, Why?

I think it's because they're delicious, she says.

Snails? he says, making a face. She watches him think. He is thinking, she can see, of the snail who would not, could not, would not, could not, would not join the dance in *Alice's Adventures in Wonderland*. The snail who refused to be thrown into the sea. It's marvelous to know another person's entire literary canon by heart. It's like knowing their secret personal language.

Later, at the restaurant with the excellent lunchtime

prix fixe, the older boy is made jealous by the little one's adroit handling of his mussels, plucking out one fat bite after the other, and he leans forward and says, Those were alive, too. But now they're dead. You're eating dead things. Dead little mussels sitting in your belly.

The little one puts down the shell he was using as picker and says, No!

Yup, the older boy says, eating calmly. Pleasure flicks over his face as he watches the little one crumble, then he laughs when the mother shoots him a furious look. He is not a sociopath, she hopes. Just an older brother. She has an older brother who has turned into a fine person, a kind doctor who takes care of veterans and has become a feminist with the arrival of daughters, but who was endlessly cruel to her as a child. Her older son is only rarely cruel.

The little boy climbs into the mother's lap and cries into her chest.

Oh, Little Bear, it's okay, she says, stroking his head. The older boy eats his little brother's french fries, another thing they never get at home.

It's not okay, the little one says. It's really not okay to eat alive things.

You don't have to if you don't want to, she says.

After some time, he calms. She carries him back home for naptime, and when she puts him into his sleeping bag, he pushes her face to one side and whispers hot and sticky in her ear, What if someone wants to eat *me*? And she can't tell him nobody would want to eat him, because it's not the truth; sometimes she herself wants to eat him, bite into his perfect soft sweetness as if he were a brioche.

Guy had three children with a woman named Joséphine Litzelmann, none of whom he recognized, all of whom died bastards without his name. How sad for those little children to be unclaimed by their father. How terribly sad for Guy, to not know how to love, not even his children. She smooths her son's hair until he naps.

She is asleep. The moon is out, the room pale. She was too tired to close the windows; she wanted the cold air. Something falls into her dream, into the middle of the floor.

It is enormous. It is the biggest seagull. He is looking at her.

She makes her body heavy and still. She barely breathes.

The bird doesn't move, just stands in the silvery light.

She wonders if it is about to speak, because that's what birds do in stories, and the language she is most fluent in is story. It would have a deep male voice. Even now, even after all she knows and has read, the default voice of stories is male. But the bird just stands there, mute.

Eventually, her eyes grow heavy and she drifts out again.

In the morning the boys creep in, their limbs cold. They stay quiet. The little boy sucks his thumb, sighing contentedly. She unpeels her eyelids with tremendous effort.

I had a dream last night, she says. An enormous bird came into the room through the skylight and stood in the middle of the floor just staring at me.

Your breath stinks, the older boy says. It's like something died in your mouth.

Can we watch *Tintin*? the little one says.

She pulls her feet under the duvet and warms them on her children's legs, and they shriek at the ice in her bones. Why the hell not, she says.

When she can gather her body enough to move, she stands. She narrowly misses stepping in a huge jellied bird poop in the middle of the floor, shining and bloodshot like an eye.

The waitress said to the mother's question that it was true, Fécamp was heavily bombed during the war.

She sounded cheerful, but must have been offended because she never came back after she delivered their food. All the mother asked was why there were almost no old buildings by the harbor; though, it's true, it may have been evident in her voice that she'd never seen such an ugly city as this one.

The day is tannic in color. The beach's curve between the cliffs is much larger here, dwarfing the cliffs themselves so they seem an afterthought. On one end of the boardwalk, they had seen a carnival covered in tarps. The carnies smoked cigarettes moodily in their plastic chairs.

The boys begged to see the rides, but the carnival didn't open until afternoon, and the mother thought she'd probably die of sadness if she were to stay in this town for that long. She dragged her boys into a restaurant that looked less bad than the others.

The boys are sick of *galettes*, sick of *pommes frites*, but everything else on the menu was once alive, and she capitulates; she has no more strength, she lets them eat pistachio ice cream for lunch. Each bowl comes with tiny lit sparklers, and her sons' faces open, momentarily happy. She drinks a pitcher of cider and picks at her scorched omelet.

On the long boardwalk, the same flags that exist everywhere up and down the coast whip and snap in the wild wind, in the dirty sky.

The tourists in the town seem morose, hurry into the restaurants, warm their hands on copper pots full of mussels in creamy sauces, barely speak to one another.

She is a shy person, but she has an urge to pull a chair up to any of these tables with their glum diners, to speak breathlessly about anything, about politics or money or God, anything adult, to bend her tongue toward thought. Solitude is danger for a working mind. We need to keep around us people who think and speak.

When we are lonely for a long time, we people the void with phantoms. Guy said this, in "Le Horla."

Every hundred feet down the boardwalk are tiny perfect playgrounds, and she decides to turn the day into a workout day to keep it from being a total wash. The other parents watch her from the corners of their eyes, weirded out, as she does crunches and pull-ups and push-ups and runs in place while the boys scream and climb the equipment and play hide-and-seek, ignoring all of the other children.

None of the little shacks on the boardwalk are open, but she still reads the offerings on their placards as she counts out squat-jumps.

A *coupe américaine* is an ice cream with eight different flavors, whipped cream, a banana, and three separate kinds of sauce.

A *hot-dog américain* is a foot-long sausage in a half baguette, covered in toasted Gruyère.

A three-foot whip of multicolored licorice stuffed with colorful cream is called a *réglisse américaine*.

All things nauseating and deadly are American, apparently.

Well, okay, she can't disagree.

They leapfrog on down the string of playgrounds. Despite the cold, she begins to sweat, and so do the boys. The sun comes weakly out and the brown fades into pale.

God, I'm lonely, she thinks.

They arrive at a lighthouse at the end of a channel where great ships, all rust and gunmetal gray, are drawn into the relative safety of the town to rest. The armpit where the pier comes off the edge of the channel and extends into the sea is host to waves gone crazy, deadly. The *galet* stones leap like salmon. If a person were to wade in, she'd be brained. The sound of the waves withdrawing is like deafening applause. The mother feels giddy from the exercise and bows, thank you, thank you, but the boys don't laugh. They stand watching the leaping stones for a long time, and then she looks at the map on her phone and crows. Look! she tells them, gesturing up the harbor at a little cluster of nineteenth-century houses on the other side of the channel, which huddle together, distrustful of the twenty-first-century industry around them.

That house there—she points at Quai Guy de Maupassant—is where a lot of people say that Guy de Maupassant was actually born. Nobody really knows, though. His mother had been ambitious, had rented out a château, the Château de Miromesnil; we're going to go stay there when we're done with Yport—

I'm done with Yport, the older boy says.

Me too! the little boy says.

—anyway, his mother said he was born at Miromesnil, but other people said he was actually born here, that she only pretended because she was a horrible snob.

Guy, Guy, Guy, the older boy says. That's all you ever talk about.

I don't even know who Guy de Whatwhat is, the little one says.

I don't even care, the older one says.

I don't even care neither, the little one says. He looks at his mother from the corner of his eye and says, I *hate* him.

Me too, the older boy says.

Hate? the mother says, and as she says it, she understands that she also hates Guy, that despite the fact that she's been trying to write about him for a decade, what she feels is no longer love, it is hatred; it's as simple as that, that this man had no morals at all, that he was the antithesis of everything she loves and holds dear in both men and literature. She has hated him, in fact, for a long time. Since, at least, the moment she read about in the biographies when Guy was just a young man, working at the Ministry of the Marine, going off on the weekends with his dissipated friends to row and fuck and eat fried food on the Seine. There was another man who wanted to be a part of the little fraternity, a man as soft and pale as tallow, and for boys as wicked as Guy and his friends, this man was prey. They hated him. They called him *Moule à b.*, an obscenity, equal to something like Cunt Face.

So they decided to haze the hanger-on. They waited for nightfall. Then they held Cunt Face down. First, they masturbated him with fencing gloves. Second, they stuck a ruler up his rectum. He died three days later at his desk. It was not entirely clear if he died from the injuries sustained from his hazing. That's when Guy wrote a letter to his friend: Great news!!!! Cunt Face is dead! Dead on the field of battle, which is to say his fat bureaucratic ass, at about three p.m. on Saturday. His boss called for him, and when the intern entered, he found the poor little body motionless, his nose in his inkpot. They tried artificial respiration, but he never regained consciousness. They were all distraught at the Ministry of the Marine, and some said that it was *our persecution* that shortened his days . . . dead, dead dead; what a dense and wonderful word; dead, no joke, he's dead, dead. Our Cunt Face exists no more. Kicked the bucket. Killed. Kilt in his sissy kilt. Did he, at the very least, kill himself?

I also hate Guy de Maupassant, the mother says in a low voice.

The boys look at her with surprise. *Hate* is the worst swear word they know.

Why are we even here, then? says the older boy. If you hate Guy Manperson so much? I don't get it.

Are you mad at Daddy? the little boy says.

Oh my God, no, she says. Then she remembers that she is supposed to only tell the truth and says, I mean, no more than usual.

Then why are we here, the older boy says.

She counts on her fingers: One, to help you learn French. Two, to do research on Guy, whom we all hate. Three, to get away from Florida in the summer because the heat makes me want to die.

She doesn't say, Four, because there has been something heavy on her heart that she was hoping to remove by running away to France.

Well, the cold makes *me* want to die, says the older boy. I hate France.

She sighs.

I want Daddy, the little one says. I want my friends and my grandma and my daddy and my summer camp. It's pirate week! he says. I think.

The older boy puts an arm around his brother. It's always pirate week at summer camp, he says sadly.

They have tickets for the carousel, but the boys are too glum to ride.

They will only sit in plastic chairs, watching other children spin over and over. They have rimmed their mouths in green pistachio ice cream.

Well, at least the mother had an entire carafe of rosé at dinner and the pounding music is drowning out the seabirds. The sky is already red: sunset will take hours tonight. She feels untethered. She sits beside her sons watching a little band of six or so dirty blond children who are playing on the seawall. Every one of their heads is buzzed, and half have a slick of snot from nose to chin. A few, she thinks, are girls. There are placeholder nubs for boobs.

An infinite weariness comes over the mother as she

watches these children's bodies leap off the seawall. They glow palely, like angels, she thinks. Maybe it's just malnutrition.

She can't stop the thought that children born now will be the last generation of humans. Her sons have known only luck so far, though suffering will surely come for them. She feels it nearing, the midnight of humanity. Their world is so full of beauty, the last terrible flash of beauty before the long darkness.

Refusing the pleasure of a dusk like tonight's with its cool wind, its sunset, its ocean, its carousel, its ice cream, strikes her as profoundly immoral.

Now a hunger that cannot quite be located in the body comes over her, a sense of yearning, for what? Maybe for kindness, for a moral sense that is clear and loud and greater than she is, something that can blanket her, no, no, something in which she can hide for a minute and be safe.

So she stands tipsily and walks to the clump of children on the seawall and gives a nub-chested one the laminated tickets for the carousel. The child looks at the mother briefly, shoots her a gappy grin, jumps down off the seawall. The rest of the urchins follow.

And then the mother watches the little cluster run to the woman who takes the tickets, and this blonde, big-busted woman frowns at them and snatches the tickets from their hands, muttering something, then the girl says something, and the other woman looks up at the mother across the spinning carousel, and her face is folded in contempt. The buzz-cut children don't get on the carousel. They run off.

The mother understands then that she is a fool. Those are the carousel lady's own children. The mother watches as the other woman turns away, knowing before she even looks that her own smaller son will have begun to cry because she has given away their tickets, and the older one's face will be aghast, another failure of hers that sinks to the bottom of him and that he will never forget.

They've been in Yport for ten days when, at last, she notices that there is a placard announcing free wifi in the tiny square outside the church.

She makes the older boy read a book to the little one, and he murmurs away on the curb beside her because the only bench is already occupied by pigeons and a snoozing woman.

She has thousands of emails. She goes through quickly, gets rid of the spam, the people who want things from her, notices from the boys' schools, notes from her benign stalkers. Business she puts in a folder for later, or maybe never.

There are ten messages from her husband with swiftly breeding exclamation points.

She tries Skype, muting it to keep from getting her sons' hopes up, but her husband doesn't answer, and in retaliation, she won't answer his emails. Let him dangle.

And then there are five emails from different people, all of which have the same friend's name in the subject line. This friend is the sweetest man alive. He is slender, humble, vegan, bearded; he has tattoos he drew himself in his punk-rock-commune youth; he is now a librarian, a cartoonist, a fellow writer. She always thought that he is maybe too kind to ever be a great writer, but perhaps that will change with age; she knows from personal experience that most people get meaner when they get older. Once, she was having a terrible day and he was riding his bicycle and stopped when he saw her and she confessed her sadness, her sense of futility and the doom lurking around the corner, and he hugged her, and that night he left an entire vegan chocolate cake on her front step. After her husband went to bed, she ate half of it, and although she immediately felt much worse, the friend's kindness in the moment when she opened the shoe box and saw the beautiful shining vegan buttercream inside made her feel loved.

A year ago, she went to his wedding in South Florida, where he married his high school sweetheart, who was tattooed all over like him, a thin Bettie Page in red lipstick and a white halter dress. They moved away from Florida to Philadelphia. He had a new baby. They gave the baby the name of a character from the mother's last book, in fact the strongest, toughest, best character in the book, the nexus of her community, though the naming might have been a coincidence.

The emails all say the same thing: that this good and quiet man has killed himself.

There is a sucking sound. When she looks up, the edges of the little square have blurred. It is here again. It has found her again, the dread, in Yport, this place that she thought would be too small to be noticed.

When the mother and her boys come home to Florida, there will be a memorial service in the Thomas Center atrium and the mother will stand in the heat against a cool stone pillar and feel shy in the presence of such collective grief. Her friend's widow and her teenaged daughter from a different marriage will be there; the baby will be there. The mother will touch the baby's perfect head and feel her warmth. And then she'll remember the flash of gratitude and understand the harm she's done the baby in that moment, the sin of relief that the terrible thing happened on the mother's periphery, not at her center. Because this is a grief that she could survive.

She moves over to her children and puts an arm around both. They let her hold them, wondering. They smell mealy and could do with a shower, and she should probably toss these rotten shoes. But oh, God, she thinks. Let them stink.

The mother and her sons go back to Paris for their last week in France.

But first, they pack up the Yport house and drive to

Dieppe, still scarred from World War II. Dieppe is not far at all from Calais, where, she'll read later, migrants are massing into a giant camp called the Jungle, waiting for passage to England. In their little Mercedes, the mother and the boys see none of these desperate people. The Norman countryside looks oddly depopulated. They drive down narrow roads through green and gold fields, through towns luxurious in their flowers and cleanliness, to the Château de Miromesnil, where they stay in a tower room, fragrant and clean and white and peaceful and expensive. This is the place where Guy was born, though she finds that she could give no fucks at all about him anymore.

After the constant noise of the sea, the gulls and the waves and the music and the tourists, the château in the warmth of its fields is almost eerily quiet.

The birds sing, but songs. The gardens are vast and dreamy, giant *potagers* so perfectly kept it makes the mother cry with misplaced tenderness. There's a wall of espaliered pear trees, heavy with almost-ripe fruit. A kind of miniature apple tree that was trained on a knee-high vine. Black dahlias, glossy eggplants, butterflies an impossible shade of minty green. The boys swing the ancient bell in the chapel, pulling on the rope with all the strength in their bodies. She takes pictures of them with a mossy stone bust of Guy de Maupassant, and in every picture, the older son scowls.

There are no restaurants anywhere near for dinner that night, and the only place open within ten kilometers is a bakery, so they buy what is left, pastries and bread and jam, and eat in the garden, with the last of the visitors strolling through.

The boys run up and down the long alleys, careful children, touching nothing, ruining nothing. Good, smart boys. There will still be time, perhaps, at least she hopes, to make them into good men. They run back to her to finish their milk, to throw their arms around her, perhaps relieved that they aren't so cold anymore. An apple falls on the older son's head, and he looks betrayed at her, that she'd let this happen, then he relents and laughs.

There is a storm in the night, the trees lashing in the dark garden, the boys on the floor in the sleeping bags and the mother penned up with them.

The mother cannot sleep and she thinks of Laure Le Poittevin, Guy's mother. How terrible for her to outlive her two sons, both of whom died very young of secretive sex leading to syphilis, which spread through their bodies and cracked into insanity. How lonely it would be, the mother thinks, looking at her children, to live in this dark world without them.

She watches as the new light in the morning wakes them up. She is so weary. Her sons belong in their own beds. She doesn't belong in France, perhaps she never did; she was always simply her flawed and neurotic self, even in French. Of all the places in the world, she belongs in Florida. How dispiriting, to learn this of herself.

And yet this will not be what defines the trip.
   Two things will stay longer.

The first is their last night in Yport, coming up from salted caramel crêpes, when the mother sees a man picking up jars from a box at his feet and heaving them into a great green container beside the casino. She laughs aloud. Recycling. Of course. When the boys are finally asleep and the streets have gone quiet, she hangs her arms with plastic bags full of bottles and runs as fast as she can down the hill, holding her breath against fire in the house or one of the boys waking in a terror and calling for her and finding nothing where she is supposed to be.

She throws the glass in all at once and bolts home. The boys are asleep, safe in their beds.

At midnight, as she finishes the last bottle of wine in the house and continues to write nothing at all, there is a knock on the door. She feels courageous, almost light, and opens it angrily. Jean-Paul is on the step, fist raised to knock, so it looks as if he is punching. She almost ducks. He seems bashful and holds another folded paper in his hand.

He pardons himself, hopes they had a pleasant stay, has something for the mother but she isn't supposed to read it until he has left.

He found the mother, he says, very sympathetic.

She is far from sympathetic.

He puts the paper in her hand, squeezes it, and is gone.

It is a poem, in rhyme. It is about the mother.

She doesn't read more than the first stanza, though she can't bring herself to throw out the poem.

She starts laughing and can't stop, even when her stomach hurts, even when her sight goes glossy. Another fucking writer; just what the world needs.

And this moment will be the one to stay with her forever: She's crouching beside her smallest son in the exposed seabed. The tide pool a miniature ocean. A snail retreats his horns when they tickle him with a feather, a red anemone pulses as the tide pulls the water away, algae with green hairs feel like satin on their fingertips. The little boy is still, sun on his brown body. The older boy is picking across the rocks, toward the cliffs. He is the size of her palm. Soon she'll call him back. Not yet.

The little one and she watch ghostly things with silver backbones nibbling at their ankles. Shrimp or fish, she doesn't know. She knows so little about this astonishing world.

If a meteor crashed down right now, would we die? the little boy says.

Depends on the meteor, I guess, she says.

Huge.

Then probably, she says very slowly.

He sucks his lips in. Like the dinosaurs, he says.

The truth might be moral, but it isn't always right. She says, Well. The plus side is that we'd never know about it. One minute, we're in the sun, enjoying the ocean and ice cream and naps and love. The next, nothing.

Or heaven, he says.

Okay, she says sadly.

The older boy is now the size of a thumb. He has gone too far for her to save him in a calamity. Rogue wave, kidnapper. But the mother doesn't call for him. There is something so resolute in the set of his shoulders. He isn't going anywhere, just away. She understands.

When she looks back at her younger son, he is holding a rock over his head. He is aiming at the snail. Boom, he whispers, but he keeps his arm in the air. And he holds his fingers closed.

ACKNOWLEDGMENTS

Thank you: Florida, sunniest and strangest of states; Bill Clegg and Marion Duvert; Sarah McGrath, Jynne Dilling Martin, Danya Kukafka, Geoff Kloske, Anna Jardine, and the rest of the shining lights at Riverhead; Kevin A. González, Elliott Holt, Ashley Warlick, and Laura van den Berg; the editors of the journals and anthologies where these stories first appeared; the MacDowell Colony for the gift of time; Ragdale and Olivia Varones; my parents and parents-in-law; and the nannies and teachers and copy editors and good dogs and friends and readers of the world.

Thank you, Clay and Beckett. Extra thanks to Heath, my Florida baby, whose book this is.

Lauren Groff's first novel, *The Monsters of Templeton*, published when she was twenty-nine, was not only an immediate *New York Times* bestseller; it was the beginning of what would become one of the most important careers of her generation. Today, Groff is understood to be "a writer of rare gifts" (*The New York Times Book Review*), "one of the best writers in the United States" (*Los Angeles Review of Books*), and someone whose work is "epically transfiguring" (*The New Yorker*).

A two-time finalist for the National Book Award, Groff has won the PEN/O. Henry Award and been a finalist for the National Book Critics Circle Award. And she was named one of *Granta*'s Best of Young American Novelists for 2017.

Across all of her novels and story collections, whether writing about the dynamics between lovers, siblings, friends, or strangers meeting for the first time, Lauren Groff combines powerful language with empathetic characters and gripping storytelling, to create worlds that are vivid, complex, and unusual.

"Even from her impossibly high starting point, Lauren Groff just keeps getting better and better."
—*The Washington Post*

Every story has two sides. Every relationship has two perspectives. And sometimes, it turns out, the key to a great marriage is not its truths but its secrets.

At age twenty-two, Lotto and Mathilde are tall, glamorous, madly in love, and destined for greatness. A decade later, their marriage is still the envy of their friends, but with an electric thrill we understand that things are even more complicated and remarkable than they have seemed. With stunning revelations and multiple threads, and in prose that is vibrantly alive

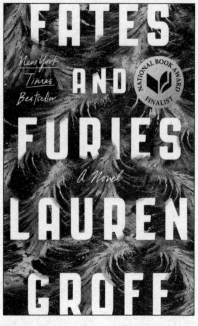

and original, Lauren Groff delivers a deeply satisfying novel about love, art, creativity, and power that is unlike anything that has come before it. Profound, surprising, propulsive, and emotionally riveting, it stirs both the mind and the heart.

"Lauren Groff is a writer of rare gifts, and *Fates and Furies* is an unabashedly ambitious novel that delivers—with comedy, tragedy, well-deployed erudition and unmistakable glimmers of brilliance throughout."

—The New York Times Book Review